THE
ELUSIVE
CHAUFFEUR

4/17/2021

To: Liz

David Brown

WHEN A MILLION-DOLLAR HEIRESS TURNS UP DEAD,
THE NUMBERS JUST DON'T ADD UP

THE
ELUSIVE
CHAUFFEUR

DAVID H. BROWN

YorkshirePublishing
www.yorkshirepublishing.com
Write Now.

ISBN: 978-1-946977-15-1
The Elusive Chauffeur
Copyright © 2008 by David H. Brown

For permission requests, write to the publisher at the address below.

Yorkshire Publishing
3207 South Norwood Avenue
Tulsa, Oklahoma 74135
www.YorkshirePublishing.com
918.394.2665

DEDICATION

This book is dedicated to the memory of my father, Elwood, and my mother, Olive.

ACKNOWLEDGMENTS

I owe a great debt to one publishing house and many people who have helped me in the publication of this novel. I am thankful to Tate Publishing & Enterprises, LLC for financially supporting my project. I also want to thank its staff for believing in my project and helping me through the publishing process.

I am indeed grateful to my friends and family who read early drafts of the manuscript and made constructive suggestions. They are David Tobin, Samuel Richbart, Kathryn Thompson, Craig Saunders, Brandon Warden, Edmund Thomas, Carol Berridge, and my daughters, Marlo and Dawn.

Finally, I want to thank my loving wife, Kay, for her many ideas and constant support. She read the manuscript almost as many times as I did.

ONE

"Let me out of here!" Samuel Mohlar yelled, as his eyes remained closed. "There's fire all around me. It's unbearably hot in here. Ken, thank God you're not in here too. Unlock the door so I can get out."

"I can't unlock it!"

"My suffering will never end unless I can get out of here. I can hear people groaning and crying, but I can't see anyone. Ken, break down that door!"

Mohlar panicked when he realized that Ken Gray couldn't break down the door. He suddenly woke shivering in a cold sweat, longing for an icy drink. As he rose from the sofa, he thought, *Why do I keep having this nightmare? I'm glad dreams rarely come true.*

After glancing at the wall clock that read 6:50, Mohlar poured himself a glass of lemonade, thinking he had plenty of time before his meeting with Raymond Clark, a prospective client. While sipping the lemonade, the image of being surrounded by fire haunted him until he remembered the wall clock was slow and Clark should have arrived ten minutes ago.

Why can't Gray put away his clothes? Mohlar thought when he saw Gray's shirt lying on the desk near the window. After Mohlar stuffed the shirt in the desk drawer, he turned and saw his reflection in the window. As he was combing his jet-black hair, he saw a taxi pull off a busy Rochester street and stop in front of his office building. A man over seven feet tall wearing a brown hat got out of the taxi. He paid the fare and walked toward Mohlar's office building.

After a few minutes, Mohlar heard a knock at the door and opened it. He looked up at the tallest man he had ever seen. He was solidly built, wide in the shoulders, had some gray in his well-trimmed hair, and looked to be in his late forties. "Hello, I'm Sam Mohlar."

The man was immaculately dressed in an expensive gray suit with no stripes or patterns. His yellow silk tie was clipped to a white shirt with a gold tie clasp. He wet his upper lip with his tongue and said, while holding out his hand, "And I'm Raymond Clark. Dr. Mohlar, I'm sorry I'm late, but I had to finish an inventory at the plastic factory I own. I always do the inventory alone after the day shift goes home." Mohlar shook Clark's hand before he entered.

As Clark passed through the doorway, his soft brown hat crushed between his head and the top of the doorframe.

"It's interesting that you do the inventory alone. My uncle who manages a warehouse always has two men do his inventories. He feels he'd get an inaccurate inventory with one man doing the job."

Clark removed his hat and smoothed his brown hair with his large hand. "If I do the inventory, I know it's accurate," Clark responded, making an emphatic gesture with his hat in his hand. "Besides, I can't see paying two people to do a job I can do by myself."

"I'm sorry that my partner, Mr. Gray, is unable to be with us tonight." Gray had a hot date, but Mohlar hid his irritation at his partner, who put his social life over his work.

"Why are you called 'doctor'?" Clark asked as he placed his hat on a hat rack.

"I have a Ph.D. in mathematics. Please call me Sam."

"The ad in the phonebook said that you do investigations of all types—divorces, child custody, missing people, accidents, surveillance, et cetera. Is that correct?"

"Yes."

Clark and Mohlar sat across from each other at his desk. After a few seconds, Clark asked, "What qualifications do you have for this type of work?"

"I assist the Rochester Police Department in homicide investigations. If someone discovers the body soon after death, I'm called in to determine the time of death. But mainly the Rochester police want me to look for clues that might help them with the murder investigation. I have a reputation with them for spotting significant details." Mohlar picked up a pen and notepad from his desk and asked, "How can I help you?"

"Find my ex-chauffeur, Richard Flood. Do you remember hearing of the death of Krista Clark that happened three days ago?"

"As I recall, she was a very wealthy woman. I believe the Rochester police determined her death was a suicide."

Clark sighed, crossed his legs, and said, "The woman was my wife. I think Flood killed her and made it look like it was a suicide."

"Why do you think Flood killed your wife?"

"Krista fired Flood eight days before her death. He was irate at her for letting him go. He had been the family chauffeur for fifteen years and thought he had been mistreated."

"Why did Krista fire Flood?"

"Flood was late picking her up to take her to an important business meeting. She was furious when she found out he was late because he was playing poker."

"Did the police find anything at the murder scene that would place Flood there?"

"No."

"Did the police ask Flood where he was when the murder happened?"

"They can't find him. But they did talk to his girlfriend and she produced an alibi for him."

Mohlar rubbed his chin and said, "You really don't have any evidence that Flood killed your wife. Suspicion without proof is a dangerous thing. You shouldn't tell anyone, except the police, what you just told me."

"Sam, if you investigate Krista's death, I think you'll find evidence that Flood was at the murder scene."

"That's possible. When we find Flood, do you want us to turn him over to the police for further investigation?"

"Yes, but I want to talk to him before you do."

Mohlar took his hand from his chin, wrote on his notepad, and then asked, "What do you want to talk to him about?"

"I'd rather not say."

"Is it because you want to kill him yourself?"

Clark leaned forward in his chair and, with hard eyes, said, "I'd like to kill him, but I'd be satisfied to witness his execution by the State of New York."

Mohlar put the tips of his fingers together and looked to be deep in thought. He wanted to express his thoughts so that they conveyed exactly what he was thinking. As a mathematician he was used to expressing himself precisely. After a minute he said, "My partner and I will only take this job under the following conditions: one, if we are convinced that Krista's death was not a suicide; two, if it was possible that Flood could've killed Krista; three, if you will not harm Flood when he's found."

"I give you my word that I will not harm Flood as long as you turn him over to the police. I'm convinced that Flood killed my wife, and you'll also be convinced once you investigate the murder. I can understand your position, but finding Flood is important to me. And I can assure you that this job will mean big money for you." Clark paused for a moment and then repeated for emphasis, "Big money."

"If we're interested in taking the job, and we can agree on our fee, I'll draw up a contract."

"I'd prefer to draw up the contract. I'll have it ready for you to sign should you decide to take this job."

"Here's my business card."

Clark took the card and said, "Flood is fifty-two, and approximately your height and weight. Here are two pictures of him. On each of the pictures I've written a description of him."

"Besides the police, who should we talk to about this case?"

Clark took his hat off the rack and replied, "Her personal secretary, Marlo Shaw, knew Krista better than anyone besides me. Marlo was the one who heard the shot that killed Krista and called the police." He put his hat on and left.

TWO

The next day Mohlar discussed with Gray his conversation with Clark. Gray was the best man Mohlar had ever known at gathering information. Once they had information concerning a case, Mohlar was better at developing theories that led to cracking the case.

Mohlar said, "There's a good chance that Clark wants us to find Flood so that he can kill him. I don't want any part of this deal if he's using us. Since Clark doesn't know you, I want you to contact him and see if you think he's angry enough at Flood to kill him."

"What does Clark look like?"

As Mohlar looked up at his six-foot-six, two hundred-fifty pound partner, he replied, "He's about a foot taller and fifty pounds heavier than you."

Boy, he must be a big dude, Gray thought.

"And what about Flood? What does he look like?"

While giving Gray one of the pictures, Mohlar said, "He's five-foot-nine, weighs one hundred-eighty pounds, has blue eyes, and is twenty years older than us."

"He looks like an older you without a beard," Gray said as he looked at the picture.

"Find out as much as you can from Marlo Shaw about this case. I'll go to police headquarters and talk to Lieutenant Luff about it."

———

When Mohlar arrived at police headquarters, he asked to see

Lieutenant Luff. In his office, Mohlar sat at Luff's desk in a thick–cushioned chair. Elwood Luff, who had been the chief homicide investigator for the city of Rochester ever since Mohlar first met him, was book smart, but not street smart. He earned two degrees in criminal justice from the University of Rochester. In homicide investigations, he was competent but not creative. He knew how to gather evidence, order laboratory tests, et cetera, but was unimaginative. Since he never could think like a criminal, the theories he formulated were always obvious. As a result, his theories were often wrong.

"Sam, what brings you to my office?" Luff asked as he sat in a swivel chair across from Mohlar.

"I'm investigating the death of Krista Clark. Why didn't you call me in on the investigation? It's now four days after her death and just about impossible for me to discover any clues."

"We didn't really need you," Luff said while running the fingers of his left hand through his thinning hair. "She committed suicide. We had no unanswered questions."

"Why do you think her death was a suicide?"

"For several reasons. First, she left a note saying she was unhappy and wanted to die. Second, we found a revolver in her hand and the bullet that killed her was fired from that revolver. Also, she was emotionally disturbed because she separated from her husband five days before her death. Furthermore, the house doors were locked and only five people have keys to the doors. If someone came in from the outside, he had to use a key to get in because there were no signs of the doors or windows being forced open."

"Who has a key to the house?"

"Raymond Clark has two keys now, his own and his wife's. His employees, Dawn Berridge and Marlo Shaw, have keys. Darren Aderman, Krista Clark's brother, has the fifth key."

"Was Sherry Summerville the medical examiner on the scene?"

"Yes, some of our report was based on her report to us."

"Did you check to see what Krista's former chauffeur, Richard Flood, was doing that night?"

While Luff swiveled his chair from side to side, he answered, "We had heard that Flood was very angry with Mrs. Clark, and we wanted to talk to him. We've been looking for him and can't find him. Our search is restricted to the city, but I don't think he's here. We talked to his girlfriend, Carol Wilson, and found out that Flood was with her at the time Mrs. Clark died. She said they went to a play that evening, and after the play he took her home."

"Do you think she was covering for him?"

He shook his head and said, "She seemed to want to fully co-operate with us."

"I'd like to talk to her."

"She lives at 315 Descartes Street."

Mohlar smiled and said, "You mispronounced the name of the street. It was named after a French mathematician and is pronounced 'day cart.' Would you like to question Flood if I can find him?"

"Yes, I would, since there was something about Wilson's statement that bothers me."

What bothers him about Wilson's statement? Mohlar thought. *I don't think I'll ask him...I'd like to get that information directly from Wilson.*

After a few seconds he said, "Did you do a background check on Flood?"

"Yes."

"What did you come up with?"

"Nothing."

"May I have a copy of the police report?"

Mohlar and Luff had been friends for about four years. Over those years Mohlar helped Luff solve many cases. Thinking his friend may once again be helpful to him, he replied, "Yes."

————

Leaving police headquarters, Mohlar called Gray to inform him of his conversation with Luff. Specifically, he wanted Gray to find out why Berridge, Shaw, and Aderman had keys to Clark's house.

Since Mohlar and Summerville had worked on many homicide cases together, Mohlar knew her well. When Summerville saw Mohlar, she smiled and said, "Nice seeing you again, Sammy."

"Elwood said you did the medical exam on Krista Clark. How sure are you that her death was a suicide?"

She sighed, then asked, "Why do you want to know?"

"Her husband asked me to find his ex-chauffeur, Richard Flood. He thinks Flood killed his wife."

Summerville no longer smiled. She went over to her file cabinet and pulled out a sheet of paper. After a few seconds of looking at it she said, "I am ninety-nine percent sure Clark's death was a suicide."

She handed Mohlar the report and sat down at a desk that had only four things on top of it: Two pens and a paperweight were on the left side and a graphing calculator was on the right side of the desk.

Mohlar recognized much of her report from the police report. While he quickly read through it, Summerville picked up a pen and nervously fiddled with it.

"Did you find any gunpowder on her head?" Mohlar inquired.

"No," she answered curtly.

"If the revolver made contact with her head, wouldn't there be powder residue on her head?"

She stuttered when answering, "Y-yes. There's no question this wound was a non-contact wound." This was the first time Mohlar had ever heard her stutter.

Mohlar watched her move the calculator from the right side of the desk to the left side. "Someone intent on killing himself would put the gun to his head and shoot. I'm starting to think Clark's death was not a suicide," the detective said.

While Summerville moved the paperweight from the left side to the right side of the desk she said, "Usually suicides by gunshot are as you described, but she could've held the gun several inches from her head and shot herself. I still stand by my report."

———

Mohlar left and drove to 315 Descartes Street. He pushed the doorbell and heard the distant chimes inside. He watched three boys pedal their ten–speed bikes past the house. He pushed it again and waited. He listened to two blue jays chirping at each other. Again he rang the doorbell. Just as he was about to leave, an attractive woman in her late twenties opened the door.

"Are you Carol Wilson?"

"No, I am not," she said as she started to close the door. She had an immature voice and her eyes were dazed as though she had been awakened from a deep sleep. Her blonde wig was slightly off center.

Mohlar placed his foot in the doorway preventing the door from closing. "Is she in the house? I'm investigating the death of Krista Clark, and I need to ask her some questions."

"Okay, I'm Carol Wilson. I don't like to talk to people I don't know, especially men. I told the police all I know. Where's your ID?" Her eyes were no longer dazed, but focused on the detective.

Mohlar opened and closed his wallet to reveal his private investigator's license and said, "I'm a friend of Lieutenant Luff, but I'm not from the Rochester Police Department. Mrs. Clark's husband has asked me to investigate the death of his wife. I won't take much of your time, and you could be a great deal of help to me."

Wilson opened the door, allowing Mohlar to enter. "I'm sorry I was rude, but girls have to be careful around strangers these days. Richard spoke well of Mr. Clark, and I'm glad to be of help to him," she said as she sat on her living room sofa.

Mohlar looked at her with eyes that weighed and judged her. The police dismissed Flood as a suspect based on her testimony, but would he?

"How long have you known Richard Flood?" Mohlar asked, pulling a thin blue pen from his shirt pocket.

She smiled slightly without separating her lips and answered, "We met about six months ago, and we've been seeing each other regularly since then."

"What kind of person is he?" Mohlar asked as he sat next to her on the sofa.

Without hesitation and with a sparkle in her eyes she said, "He's the nicest man I've ever known. He has always been gentle and kind to me."

Mohlar wondered, *Will she try to cover for Flood because she loves him?*

"I understand you went to see a play last Saturday evening with Mr. Flood. Was there any time that evening when he wasn't with you?"

She rose from the sofa and answered, "Yes, there was. At the end of the first act he said he wasn't feeling well. During the intermission, he went to the restroom. He didn't return until the third act."

"About when did he leave, and about when did he return?"

"Left about nine-thirty and returned about ten-thirty," she said, pausing between words, giving the impression she was selecting them with great care.

There's no cover-up here, Mohlar thought seriously.

"Since last Saturday, have you seen or heard from Mr. Flood?"

"No," she said sharply.

"Does it surprise you that he hasn't kept in contact with you?"

"Yes, it does. He's left for a few days at other times, but he always told me where he was going and when he'd be back."

"Where did he go the other times when he left Rochester?"

"Once he went to Pittsburgh, and twice he went to Buffalo. The purpose of these trips was always the same—to gamble."

"Did he do anything else on these trips?"

"One time he went to a large sports card show in Buffalo. He's an avid collector of sports cards."

"Do you know if he had a key to the Clark house?"

"I doubt that he did. Mrs. Clark fired him about two weeks ago."

"Here's my business card, Miss Wilson. If you think of anything you forgot to tell me, don't hesitate to give me a call," Mohlar said as he put his pen back in his shirt pocket.

"I'll do that. Also, if I hear from him, I'll let you know." She closed the door, wondering if it had been wise to tell him all this.

After Mohlar left Wilson, he checked the police report to see which theater they attended last Saturday. At the theater he talked to the employees, but no one could remember Flood. He drove to Mrs. Clark's house about twenty miles east of the theater. He estimated it would take from forty to fifty minutes to make a round trip from the theater to Clark's house.

Mohlar then returned to the office and made notes for Gray.

THREE

While Mohlar was gathering information from Luff, Summerville, and Wilson, Gray visited Clark's house. It was enormous with four white pillars in front. On the wide front porch he rang the doorbell.

An attractive short young blonde woman opened the door. "May I help you?" she asked as she looked up at the muscular ex-Marine.

"Are you Marlo Shaw?" Gray replied as he smelled the aroma of spaghetti sauce simmering on the stove.

"No, I'm the housekeeper, Dawn Berridge. Miss Shaw isn't here now, but I'm expecting her to return soon. May I help you?"

"My name is Ken Gray. Mr. Clark asked me to investigate the death of his wife. Did you know the Clarks well?"

"I knew them very well. I have worked for the Clarks for the past five years. Please follow me into the kitchen. I have something cooking on the stove."

While Gray followed Berridge along a passage, he noticed a poolroom on his right. A green felt pool table dominated the center of the room. He'd love to play a game, but not today.

Traversing the living room, Gray marveled at the art displayed on the walls. Paintings of some of the greatest artists who have ever lived—Rembrandt, Van Gogh, Monet, and Picasso—dotted the walls. The paintings would bring in millions of dollars in an auction. The ceiling of the living room was high, the carpeting deep, and the paneling dark. In the middle of the room hung a crystal chandelier that sparkled in the light.

"Was Mrs. Clark depressed the day she died?" Gray asked as they entered the spacious kitchen.

"I didn't see her the day she died, but she was in good spirits the previous day."

"Where were you the night Mrs. Clark died?"

With her eyes focused on the detective's eyes, she answered, "I have Saturdays off. Last Saturday, I went to visit my grandmother, Olive Milby, in Syracuse. I spent the day with her and got back here around midnight, just as Mrs. Clark's body was being wheeled out."

"What time did you leave your grandmother's?"

"About eight."

"Why did it take you four hours to drive about eighty miles?" Gray asked with a hint of suspicion in his voice.

"I drove along the shores of Lake Ontario," she said slowly. Her voice was placid, but her face was not. "At one of the scenic spots I got out of my car and looked at the sky. The moon was full and I could see millions of stars. I enjoyed looking at the moonlight reflecting off the water.

"After spending a half-hour looking at the lake, I drove to a small diner. I ate my dinner there, and then I drove home."

"Do you usually get home late Saturday nights?"

"I usually don't get home before eleven on Saturday nights. Everyone in the house sleeps in on Sunday mornings, so I get up later than usual, at seven-thirty, to fix breakfast."

"Do you enjoy working for the Clarks?"

"Mrs. Clark was difficult to work for. She was arrogant and never treated me with respect. In fact, the day before she died, she embarrassed me. Right in front of her dinner guests, she yelled at me for overcooking her steak. Mr. Clark was much nicer to me, and I enjoyed working for him. I felt bad when Mrs. Clark kicked him out of the house."

"Did you know Mrs. Clark's brother, Darren Aderman?"

"Yes, I know him, but I haven't seen him since his mother died four months ago. He didn't get along with Mrs. Clark."

"How do you know they didn't get along?"

As Dawn took the clean dishes out of the dishwasher and stacked them on the counter, she replied, "Marlo told me that Mrs. Clark didn't approve of her brother's marriage. She thought her sister-in-law only married her brother for his money. Fifteen years ago Mrs. Clark told her brother that, before the marriage. Ever since then, their relationship has been strained.

"Also, Mr. Aderman didn't think his mother's will was fair to him. He accused Mrs. Clark and her lawyer, William Goldberg, of tricking his mother into cutting him out of the estate."

"Did Mr. Flood get along with the Clarks?"

Her face reddening, she answered, "He felt about them pretty much the same as I did. He was very angry with Mrs. Clark when she fired him."

"Do you think Mr. Flood was so mad with Mrs. Clark that he could've killed her?"

As Dawn took plates off the stack of dishes and returned them to the dishwasher, she boldly said, "There's no way Mr. Flood could have killed Mrs. Clark. First of all, Miss Shaw always makes sure that the house doors are locked after dark, and Mr. Flood doesn't have a key. Also, he's the kindest, gentlest person I have ever known."

Why is she putting clean dishes in the dishwasher? Gray thought. *There's something fishy here.*

"So, Mr. Flood and you got along."

"Yes, we got along. He's a very nice man," she said with feeling.

"Were you more than just co-workers?"

"I'm not sure I know what you mean," she said as she turned her back on him and began stirring the spaghetti sauce.

"Did you ever date him?"

"No, and I don't want to answer any more of your questions," Dawn said with a raised voice.

"Why, do you have something to hide?"

"I have nothing to hide."

"Do you now or have you ever loved Mr. Flood?"

"I've loved him as long as I can remember. He's my father! My mother died when I was eight years old and he brought me up as a single parent!" she yelled as she turned around with a spoon in her hand, dripping spaghetti sauce on the floor.

Suddenly, Gray felt faint, and he sat down in a nearby chair. He had never been more embarrassed than he was at that moment.

He was pleased to hear the front door close and assumed that Miss Shaw had returned.

"Thank you for your help," the detective said as he got up and walked toward the front door to see who had just entered the house. Dawn didn't reply and returned to her kitchen duties.

Gray saw a slender woman, whose dark hair was threaded with gray, walking toward him. "My name is Kenneth Gray. Are you Marlo Shaw?"

"Yes, I am. Are you feeling all right? Your face seems pale. Could I get you a drink?"

"Okay."

"Would you like cranberry juice or soda?"

I'd like a shot of whisky, Gray thought, *but not now*. "Water with ice would be fine. Thanks."

Marlo went to the kitchen, leaving Gray in the living room admiring the paintings on the wall. She pulled a tray of ice cubes from the freezer, filled a glass with ice, and poured spring water into the glass. When she returned, Gray was gazing at the Picasso painting.

After a couple of swallows of water, he said, "Mr. Clark wants me to investigate the death of his wife. I've come to ask you some questions concerning the death of Mrs. Clark. I understand that you were her personal secretary and have known her for a long time."

Wow, thought Gray as he eyed her up and down, *she's a knockout for a middle-aged woman. Really stacked.*

She replied, "That's correct."

With one hand in the pocket of his slacks and the other hand holding his glass, he asked, "Could you tell me what happened the night she died?"

She changed slightly the position of the Picasso, crossed the room to a large window, opened the drapes, and sat down next to Gray. In a flirtatious way, she brushed back her hair and said softly, "Mrs. Clark and I were the only people in the house last Saturday night. We finished dinner about seven. From seven to eight we played a game of gin rummy that I won. We both retired to our bedrooms. I read until nine when I turned out my light. I was unable to sleep because of arthritic pains. After I took an aspirin, I turned on the television in my room to listen to the ten o'clock news. A couple of minutes later I heard a shot that came from the other side of the house—the side of the house where Mrs. Clark's bedroom is located. I immediately ran to Mrs. Clark's bedroom, knocked, and yelled at her door."

As tears were forming in her eyes, she pulled a tissue from her purse and rubbed her eyes. After a few seconds, she continued, her voice infused with emotion, "When I didn't hear an answer, I went into her room and saw Mrs. Clark lying face up on the floor in a puddle of blood, a revolver in her right hand. I immediately ran to the telephone and called 911. In about fifteen minutes, the police arrived. I told Lieutenant Luff everything that happened."

"How long did it take you to get from your bedroom to Mrs. Clark's bedroom?"

Sobbing she answered, "A couple of minutes. My bedroom is a fair distance from her bedroom."

"Did you see or hear anyone leaving her bedroom?"

"No," she answered.

"Did you see anything in the bedroom that would help us with this investigation?"

"There was a note on the desk next to the computer."

"Do you remember what the note said?"

She pulled a piece of paper from her purse and answered, "I copied the note. It said, 'I am going to end it all. I am a rich woman in money, but a poor woman in love. I am estranged from the only man I have ever loved. I have lost the respect of my husband, so I no longer desire to live. I am convinced that it would be futile for me to try to regain his love. I am so upset I can't continue living. I must get out of my misery. Krista Clark.'"

"Was this handwritten?"

"No." She paused, and Gray noticed her eyebrows crease in a quizzical expression. "It was typed. Even the name was typed."

There's something about that note that bothers her. Maybe she thinks that Krista didn't write the note, Gray speculated. "Did Mrs. Clark seem to be upset or worried before her death?"

"On Monday, March 21, five days before her death, she had a terrible argument with her husband. Mrs. Clark was in the living room and I was in the kitchen when he came home drunk—"

"Do you know what the argument was about?" Gray interrupted.

"At first, I couldn't tell what they were talking about. Mr. Clark slurred many of his words and sometimes talked at the same time Mrs. Clark was talking. But I could tell they were having a violent difference of opinion about something. After a few minutes, I went into the living room to see what all the commotion was about. I heard her get on him about his drinking problem."

Suddenly, an irritated tone came into her voice as she said, "I saw him lose his temper. He hit her many times and she fell to the floor. While on the floor, she told him to get out of the house and never return. She was very upset that night and was despondent for the next two days. But what seems strange to me is that his drunkenness and abuse had been going on for many years. There must have been some other reason she kicked him out."

Her voice returned to normal as she added, "But the day before her death, she seemed to be happy. She asked me if I wanted to go with her on a Caribbean cruise. When I said I wanted to go, she pulled out a bunch of pamphlets. She then showed me what we would be doing each day on the cruise."

"Did you go with Mrs. Clark on any other trips?"

"I often accompanied her on business trips, but I have never accompanied her on a pleasure trip."

"Was Mrs. Clark depressed in any way the day she died?"

"Oh no, she was in good spirits that day."

"Did you enjoy working for the Clarks?"

"It was easy working for Mrs. Clark. She treated me more like her friend than her employee. I had direct access to her any time. She even shared confidential personal and business information with me. But it was difficult working for Mr. Clark. I always felt I had to be careful what I said or what I did when he was around. If you got on his bad side, he could make life miserable for you."

"What do you mean?"

"A few years ago a young accountant working under Mr. Clark talked to him about some of their accounts. Mr. Clark told him that everything was all right, and he'd take responsibility for what happened in his department. The young accountant wasn't satisfied and talked to the owner of the company, Mrs. Aderman, Mrs. Clark's mother. She ordered the company lawyer to go over the books. Although the lawyer reported back to Mrs. Aderman that the books looked fine to him, Mr. Clark was furious at the young accountant. Mrs. Clark told me that Mr. Clark wanted to fire the accountant, but Mrs. Aderman would not allow that to happen. He told Mrs. Clark he was going to make life miserable for the young accountant. As head of the accounting department, he scheduled the work for everyone in the department. Except for the young accountant, everyone was scheduled for daytime work Monday through Friday, but he scheduled the young accountant for evening hours, Saturdays, and even some holidays. Finally the young accountant quit his job."

"What was Mrs. Clark wearing when you found her?"

"She had a nightgown on."

"So you'd say that she wasn't expecting anyone that night."

"She certainly was not expecting anyone. Her clothes were like a masterpiece of art and cost about the same. She didn't want to be seen by anyone, even me, unless she was properly dressed." With a smile on her face, she said, "She wouldn't even come down for breakfast in the morning until she looked just right."

"How long have you known Mrs. Clark?"

"I have known her for almost thirty years. We met during the first semester of our freshmen year in college. We were together in two classes. We spent many hours together that semester studying for exams. We often shared class notes to make sure we didn't miss anything important. And, as you might expect, we also shared our impressions and thoughts about attractive men on campus.

"The next semester we made sure we had all our classes together, and our friendship grew even stronger. We spent most of our time together despite the fact that we lived in different dorms. We decided at the end of our freshmen year to share the rent on an apartment. So for the last three years of college, we lived in the same apartment.

"After we graduated from college, Krista had a job waiting for her. Her family expected her to work for the family owned business after she completed college. And that was what she wanted to do."

"What was her job?"

"She was the head of the advertising department of the company."

"But I didn't have a job, so she asked me to work for her as her secretary. I couldn't have thought of a better job than working for my best friend."

"Do you know what Mr. Clark was doing last Saturday night?"

"Yes, he was the Master of Ceremony for a retirement party. A vice president of marketing for their business was retiring after working for them for thirty years. Mr. Clark wanted to make the evening a special one for him."

"How long have you known Mr. Clark?"

"Almost as long as I have known Mrs. Clark. When I was a sophomore in college, Krista's brother, Darren, introduced me to Mr. Clark. The night I met him, he asked me for a date and I accepted. We went together for about three months. I found him to be handsome and exciting to be around, but even then he had a drinking problem. When I saw he couldn't control his drinking, I broke up with him."

"Was Mr. Clark an alcoholic?" Gray asked.

"I think he was," Marlo answered. "When I was dating him, I met his family. His mother, father, and twin brothers all had drinking problems. Mr. Clark, being the youngest in his family, must have always been around booze. Ever since I've known him, he's always enjoyed drinking."

"Did Krista have a drinking problem?"

"No, she drinks—" She stopped, put her head down, and continued, "Oh, I mean, she drank in moderation.

"After Mr. Clark and I broke up, he became interested in my roommate, Krista. At first Krista refused to date him because she thought that would bother me. When I told her that I no longer had any romantic feelings toward him, she started to go out with him. They were married about two years after we graduated from college."

"How do you feel about Mr. Clark now?"

"I feel sorry for him. The sorrow he must feel over the loss of his wife must be tremendous. I'm glad he's trying to find Flood because he should have to explain to the police what he was doing last Saturday night."

"Do you think Flood could've killed Mrs. Clark?"

Marlo sharply answered, "He certainly was angry enough with Krista to have killed her. On Friday, March 18, Krista was waiting for Flood to arrive with her car to take her to a business appointment. She was angry with him because he was late—which was going to make her late. She became angrier with him when he told her he was late because he was in a poker game. Since this behavior had happened several times before, she felt justified in firing him. He thought she was being unfair because he had worked for the family for fifteen years."

"Do you know where Flood would go when he went on vacation?"

"Last summer he went to Buffalo for two weeks, and the year before he went to Pittsburgh."

"Did he have any hobbies?"

"He enjoyed gambling in all forms. He went to racetracks and casinos. He often played poker with anyone willing to play.

"He also enjoyed watching baseball, basketball, football, and hockey games. He had a large sports card collection, with an emphasis on baseball cards."

"Besides Flood, is there anyone else who doesn't like Mrs. Clark?"

"Just Mrs. Berridge and Mr. Aderman."

"Why didn't they like her?"

"Mrs. Berridge was very upset when Krista fired Mr. Flood. Also, Krista was sometimes critical of Dawn's cooking."

Marlo paused, walked over to the wall, straightened the Rembrandt painting, and then continued, "Krista and Mr. Aderman have been angry with each other almost as long as I've known them. After our freshman year of college, Krista went home for the summer. When she came back to school in September, she told me her pet dog had just died. She said that her brother was teasing her dog and the dog bit him. He became so angry at the dog that he took a four-iron from his golf bag and started beating the dog. She tried to stop him, but he pushed her aside. He continued to beat the dog until it was dead. She never forgave him for killing her dog.

"To get revenge, Krista told Mr. Aderman's girlfriend about him killing her dog. She became angry with him. Krista and Mr. Aderman have been upset with each other ever since."

"Can I look at Mrs. Clark's appointment book?"

"Go ahead," she said as she handed him the appointment book.

"I see here that two days after Mrs. Clark's death, she had an appointment to see her attorney, William Goldberg. Do you know what that was about?"

"No. Mr. Goldberg was her personal and business lawyer, so the appointment could've been about either one."

"Besides the Clarks and you, who else lives in the house?"

"Just our cook and housekeeper, Dawn Berridge."

"Was the house door locked last Saturday night?"

"Yes. Mrs. Clark always wanted me to lock the door when it got dark."

"Who has a key to the door?"

"Mr. and Mrs. Clark each had a key. Also Mrs. Berridge, Mr. Aderman, and I have keys."

"I think it's strange that Mrs. Clark's brother would have a key to the house."

"His mother lived here before she died. Toward the end, she needed almost constant care. When we weren't able to be here, Mr. Aderman would come over, let himself in by using his key, and take care of her. She died about four months ago, but as far as I know he hasn't returned the key yet."

"Why didn't they hire nurses to take care of her?"

"They hired a nurse once, but Mrs. Aderman insisted on a family member being here with the nurse. So they let the nurse go, and the family took care of her."

"Do you know where I can find Mr. Clark?"

"He's been living downtown at the Vanderbilt Hotel since he left the house. He called me yesterday and said that he would move back here in a few days."

After Gray thanked Marlo for helping him, he saw a worried look on her face. He suspected she was concerned that she had told him too much. Often women told Gray more than they intended to. Maybe it was because he was a tall, muscular, and handsome man. Probably it was because he intently listened to everything they said.

"Now I can't believe I've told so many private, personal things to a complete stranger. Mr. Gray, please don't tell Mr. Clark or Mr. Aderman anything I told you. Right now, I don't know what my job is in the company. If they find out some of the things I told you, they'll let me go."

"I won't tell anyone what we talked about, except my business partner. I'll ask him to make sure people don't know you talked to me. He's good about keeping secrets," Gray said just before departing for the Vanderbilt Hotel.

FOUR

After Gray left the Clark house, he telephoned Mohlar to let him know that he was going to the Vanderbilt Hotel to see Clark. They briefly exchanged information about the case. Gray thought, *Boy, it sure looks like we're getting close to taking this case.*

Gray arrived at the Vanderbilt Hotel within fifteen minutes of his departure from Clark's house. As Gray approached the registration desk, the clerk looked curiously at him through thick glasses and asked, "May I help you?"

"What room is Raymond Clark in?"

"I know Mr. Clark isn't in his room now. About ten minutes ago I saw him go into the poolroom. He'll be easy to spot; he's wearing a red shirt and yellow slacks."

This description of Clark was useless to Gray because he was colorblind, but he knew what Clark looked like from Mohlar's description.

Two minutes later Gray entered a large poolroom with ten tables. Although there were many people in the room, Clark was playing pool at a table by himself. After each shot, he took a swallow of beer.

When Gray was young, he spent most afternoons playing pool. He became so good that no one he played could beat him. *Why did he sink the six ball?* Gray thought. *That was the best ball for the break. I can beat this guy, no sweat.*

After observing Clark for about fifteen minutes, Gray walked up to him and said, "My name is Michael Streeter. Can I ask you a few questions about the death of your wife?"

Clark answered in an angry tone, "I don't want to talk about that, and I don't want to talk to you."

"It'll only take a few minutes of your time, and it would help me out a whole lot."

Clark glared at him with hard eyes. "Leave me alone! I told you I don't want to talk to you," he said as he moved around the pool table so that his back would be to Gray.

"I seen that you play a good game of pool," Gray said as he moved around Clark so he could look him in the eye. "How 'bout a bet? If I beat you in a game of straight pool, you gotta answer my questions honestly. But if you beat me, I'll give you a Benjamin and leave you alone."

"What do you mean, 'a Benjamin'?"

"One hundred dollars," Gray replied.

Clark was silent for a few seconds while he flicked out his tongue and wet his lips. "Streeter, I should warn you that I'm the best pool player in Rochester."

"You're wrong, Clark. I am."

Clark finished his bottle of beer and said, "Make that ten thousand dollars and have at least two people witness this bet and it's a deal."

Gray thought, *Don't laugh or he may not cooperate with you. As long as we take this case, win or lose, it don't cost me anything. If Clark beats me, Sam will add ten grand to our expense account.* "That's all right with me, but I get twenty-four hours to get the money," Gray replied with a slight smile on his face.

They then found two men in the poolroom willing to witness the bet. After they discussed the details of the bet with the witnesses, Gray asked one of the witnesses, "What's your name?"

"My name is Richard Berkhouse, but everyone calls me Rick." He pointed to the other witness and said, "He's my friend, Jerry Shoemaker."

The bet caught the attention of everyone in the room. They gathered around Gray, Clark, and the two witnesses.

"I want to make sure you're both clear on the details of this bet," Berkhouse said. "You're going to play one game of straight pool. You must call each shot you attempt. Each successful shot is worth a point. The first person to reach an agreed-upon number of points wins. If Clark wins, Streeter must return here within twenty-four hours with ten grand. If Streeter wins, Clark must answer Streeter's questions, which should only take a few minutes. How many points are needed to win?"

"I usually play to one hundred and fifty points," Gray answered.

"That's okay with me," Clark responded as he lit a cigarette. With a cigarette in one hand, his lighter in the other hand, he said, "If I should win, I'll pay Rick and Jerry one hundred dollars each to go with Streeter when he gets the money. I want to make sure Streeter comes back with the money."

Smiling, the witnesses agreed to Clark's request. Then Shoemaker said, "If Streeter wins, how many minutes does he have to question Clark?"

As Clark was setting his cigarette on an ashtray, Gray said, "If I win, ten minutes should be enough time to ask Clark all the questions I got."

Clark agreed to answer Gray's questions for ten minutes.

They lagged for break, and Gray clearly won. "I'll let you break," the detective said.

Clark racked up the fifteen balls and chalked his cue tip. "I'll play safe."

Clark asked Shoemaker to get him a quart of Mogan David Wine and a glass filled with ice. He gave him a fifty-dollar bill and told him to keep the change.

Clark stroked the cue ball and it rolled into the rack of balls. Two balls rolled out from the rack, hit the rail, and rolled toward the other balls. Clark had skillfully left the cue ball a couple of inches from the rail. He left only a bare edge of a corner ball, the four ball, sticking out from the rack of balls for Gray to shoot at. "I didn't leave you much," Clark said with a smile on his face.

Gray chalked his cue as he walked to the table. The break was good, and Gray's first reaction was to play it safe. He didn't want to take a chance on leaving Clark an opportunity of running many racks of balls. He thought he could stroke the cue ball in such a way that it would hit the four ball and send it to the end rail, but making the cue ball come to rest so that Clark would not have a shot he could make.

Gray then took a minute to consider another option. He looked very carefully at the four. Although the shot would be difficult, he could make it provided he was skillful enough. If he were to cut the four ball very precisely, it might fall in the pocket. And if he stroked the cue ball hard enough, the cue ball would split open the rack of balls, making it possible to score many points.

Gray said, "You left me enough."

He pointed to a pocket and said, "Four ball in that pocket."

He scissored his cue stick between fingers of his left hand, bent over, took careful and dead aim, and shot. The cue ball did exactly what he intended it to do. It clipped the edge of the four ball, sending it across the table and directly into the designated pocket. The cue ball smacked into the triangle of balls, spreading them apart. When the balls came to rest, the numbered balls surrounded the cue ball nicely. He looked at the result and thought about how much fun it was going to be shooting the balls into the pockets.

Gray broadly and confidently smiled while turning to Clark and said, "You may not get another shot." Clark had a worried look on his face. He did not reply.

Gray sank ball after ball of the first rack until he had one ball left. The three ball was close to the corner pocket and on the left side of Gray. While Berkhouse was racking up the fourteen-pocketed balls, the detective asked, "What do you do for a living, Clark?"

"Aren't we playing this game to give you the right to question me? If you beat me, I'll answer that question, but not before."

Gray then said, "Three ball in the corner pocket." He took aim and pocketed the three ball in the corner pocket. The cue ball crashed into the racked fourteen balls. The balls spread throughout the table.

A minute later Shoemaker returned with the wine, and Clark sat down, thinking it would be a long time before he had a chance to play. Clark thanked him for the wine and he poured it in the glass filled with ice.

Gray's play reminded everyone of a machine. Flawlessly he ran rack after rack of balls. After he had made one hundred and ten consecutive shots, Clark said, "Don't you ever miss?"

"Not very often," Gray replied.

While Gray was walking around the table, he noticed an attractive young woman watching the game. She must have just arrived because he had not noticed her before. She had a beautiful face that only showed a hint of rouge, but there was plenty of lipstick on her mouth. Gray's eyes lowered to her full figure. She was wearing a low-cut red blouse. He smiled at her as he passed in front of her. She smiled back as she selected a new, high-backed brown leather chair to sit in.

After she sat down, she pulled her skirt four inches above her knees and crossed her legs. She leaned back so her long blonde hair hung over the brown leather chair. Her brown eyes focused on Gray's face.

While Gray was lining up the next shot, his mind was on the girl in the red blouse. "Eleven ball in the corner pocket," Gray said as he drew back the cue.

He gently stroked the cue ball, and the cue ball hit the eleven. The eleven ball rolled down the table less than an inch closer to the rail than Gray had intended. It caught the corner of the pocket, bounced back and forth for a moment, and then became still. To everyone's surprise, the ball didn't go in the pocket.

After taking a sip of wine, Clark said, "You missed an easy shot."

Gray kicked a chair. "I wasn't focused on the shot," he responded.

Suddenly, Clark came to life. He began chalking his cue tip deliberately, as if he were saying to himself that he was going to run one hundred and fifty balls for the win.

Gray sat down next to the beautiful girl and looked at her. He surveyed her with eyes that took in every detail of her appearance. "My name is Michael Streeter. What's your name?" Gray whispered.

"Renee Hepler. You play a good game of straights," she whispered while her admiring brown eyes remained fastened on Gray's face.

"Clark was right. I just missed an easy shot. It might cost me the game."

"Is he better than you?"

Gray grinned and said, "He's good, but I'm better. However, just because I'm better than him doesn't mean I'll win this game. He might get in a rhythm and make one hundred and fifty shots."

Clark played well. He sank rack after rack of balls. Every shot was made with a smooth level of motion of the cue stick. Every four or five shots he stopped long enough to stroke the tip of his cue stick gently with the chalk.

"He knows what he's doing," Gray whispered to Renee. "He's big, but he moves around the table like a gymnast. He's shooting the balls in the right order. I need him to mess up."

A few minutes later Clark made the ten ball, leaving three other balls on the table. Gray whispered, "I think he made the mistake I was looking for. He should've left the ten ball for his break ball. But he might be good enough to make up for his mistake."

Clark pocketed two of the three balls left on the table. Berkhouse racked up the fourteen pocketed balls. Clark failed to pocket the break ball, but he succeeded in sending the cue ball into the fourteen racked balls to spread them throughout the table.

Berkhouse announced, "Streeter now has one hundred and ten points and Clark has eighty-six. It's now Streeter's shot."

Gray said confidently to Hepler, "Renee, I'm gonna score the next forty points. Can I talk to you after the game?"

"I'll be here," Renee responded.

"Will you get up here and shoot pool?" Clark said impatiently.

"Cool it, man. I'm coming."

Gray approached the table determined to put Renee out of his mind and to focus on the game. He wasn't even going to look at her.

Gray picked up right where he left off before he missed that easy shot on the eleven ball. He made shot after shot. He had a sense of the movement of the balls. He knew how every ball would roll even before shooting and exactly how every shot must be made. After Gray sank the next thirty-five shots, he said, "Eight ball in the corner pocket."

He had to stretch to reach the cue ball. He placed his bridge hand on the table and his other hand on the butt of the cue with his long, powerful fingers wrapped around the stick. He gently pushed the thin shaft into the cue ball.

"Foul!" Clark yelled as the cue ball rolled toward the eight ball. "Did you see that? His feet came off the floor."

The cue ball hit the eight, and the eight ball, black and silent, rolled up the green table and into the corner pocket. Now everyone was wondering if this point would count. If Gray's feet left the floor, the point would not count and the next shot would be Clark's.

"What? My feet were on the floor the whole time I shot the ball," Gray claimed.

Berkhouse and Shoemaker said that they didn't see his feet leave the floor and called the ball fair. The shot counted.

"Did anyone see his feet leave the floor?" Clark asked in an irritated tone.

After five seconds of silence, Berkhouse said, "Streeter, resume play."

Clark kicked over one chair and sat in another.

Gray sank the next four balls to win the game.

Renee came over to Gray. "Congratulations, Michael. I like men who know how to play pool. Especially winners like you."

"Thanks. I need to talk to Clark for a few minutes. Where do you live? Maybe we can hang out later."

"I'm staying at this hotel. My room number is 359. I'd like to see you later. Or call me. My extension at the hotel is the same as my room number," Renee said as she handed Gray a hotel card with the hotel's phone number on it. Gray had a wolfish smile on his face as he put the card in his pocket.

After Renee left, Clark walked over to Gray. While trying to smile, Clark said, "You play a very good game of pool, Streeter. Where did you learn to play pool?"

"When I was in high school, I went to the YMCA every day after school. I played pool there till dinnertime. Let's go to the lounge. I got some questions to ask you."

Clark said, "I think I owe you something besides my time for having beaten me. Let me buy you a sandwich and drink at a restaurant down the street."

Gray accepted the offer. After they were served their sandwiches and drinks, Clark said bluntly to Gray, "Who are you, Streeter, and why do you want me to answer questions concerning my wife's death?"

"I'm supposed to be the one asking the questions, but I'll answer you anyway. I write mystery novels, and I'm always looking for ideas for my novels. When I read about your wife's death in the paper, I wondered if she was murdered and it was made to look like a suicide. I often wonder if suicides are camouflaged murders. So I asked a friend who investigated her death to tell me what he knew. Based on what he told me, I think she was murdered. Since she was in good spirits just before she died, I think we can rule out that she committed suicide. I'd like to solve this mystery and figure out who killed your wife. To do this, I need your help.

"I'm going to mention some names of people you know. Tell me the first thing that comes to mind with each person.

"Dawn Berridge."

"Mrs. Berridge is a nice person, excellent cook, and housekeeper."

"Marlo Shaw."

"Miss Shaw was my wife's best friend. She's an excellent secretary, and I hope she'll continue to work for me."

"William Goldberg."

Clark's eyes were uneasy as he answered, "I didn't know Mr. Goldberg very well, but my wife thought of him more like her friend than her lawyer. He handled all of her legal affairs."

"Was Mr. Goldberg your lawyer?"

"I had a lawyer, Mr. Carter, before I married Krista. I hire him to do all my legal work."

"Darren Aderman."

"Darren is more of a friend than a brother-in-law. We've known each other for thirty years—ever since we played basketball together in college. I played center and he was my point guard. He and Krista certainly didn't get along. He was furious when she hired a Jew, Goldberg, as her lawyer. He's very bigoted against Jews and would just as soon kill one as to look at one."

"Krista Clark."

"Krista was the nicest woman I've ever known," Clark said in a very low tone of voice. "I didn't deserve such a good woman to be my wife." Gray could see tears in Clark's eyes when he said, "And now she's in the cold ground. I'm trying to get over losing her, but it'll take time."

"Richard Flood."

"I think Flood killed my wife, and that is why no one can find him," Clark angrily said. "I'm so convinced he killed my wife that I have two detectives looking for him. He hated my wife, and then, when he had a chance, he shot her through the head."

"If Flood killed your wife, how'd he get into the house? The doors were locked and he didn't have a key."

"I don't know. Maybe his daughter, Mrs. Berridge, let him in, or maybe she gave him her key."

"What would you do to him if you found him?"

Clark answered with no emotion in his voice, "I want to see

him dead for what he did, but, of course, I want it done legally. I have faith in our legal system."

Not wanting to discuss his wife's murder anymore, Clark said, "I'm curious about one thing, Streeter. What made you so confident that you could beat me?"

"Before I talked to you, I watched you play pool. I seen that sometimes the order in which you ran a rack of balls was not the best. Actually, you played better in the game than I thought. I best not say anymore because I might want to play you again sometime."

Gray took care of the tip and left.

FIVE

The next morning, Gray walked into his office and found Mohlar sleeping on the sofa, talking to an invisible person. Mohlar said, "It's pitch black in here and I can't see anything. Instead of groaning and crying, help me get some light in this room. Oh no! A fire with bright red flames just started. I can see a door thirty feet away, but I still can't see you. I can't move toward the door and I can't put out the fire. If it spreads, we'll die. Help me!"

Mohlar was silent for a few seconds while he turned over so his face was pointing toward the ceiling. With perspiration on his forehead, Mohlar continued, "Look, the door is opening and there's Ken on the other side. Ken, Ken!" he shouted, "I can't move. Help get me out of here!"

When Gray heard his name called, he grabbed Mohlar's arm and shook it until he woke. Mohlar sat up, looking dazed; he placed his hands over his eyes.

"Man, did you have a whopper of a nightmare. Do you know that you dream in color? I don't ever dream in color. That shouldn't be surprising—I don't see colors even when I'm awake."

Mohlar removed his hands from his face and said, "The only colors I dream in are red and black. What bothers me is that I keep having the same nightmare. I'm always in a fiery room with no way of getting out."

Gray said, "While I was on the bus the other day, I overheard some people talking about what colors mean in a dream. They were saying that if you dream in red, it means you are excited, just like in your dream. When you seen the red flames of the fire, you were excited and wanted to spring into action to put out the fire. Black means you were afraid. When you dreamt you were in the dark room, you probably were afraid of the man who was crying. Maybe in your life you have a fear of the unknown. You should get some professional help before these nightmares drive you crazy."

"Sometime…maybe," he said with a shudder.

He tried to bring his mind into focus, but he kept recalling the hot flames. He cleared his throat, gave himself a mental shakedown, and decided to push the dream to the back of his mind.

"I could use a drink," Mohlar said, forcing a smile. "Do you want a soda while we share our notes from yesterday?"

"Root beer, please."

Mohlar opened a pair of cold sodas, handed one to Gray, then sat in his swivel chair and tried to collect his thoughts. His hands were still shaking as he picked up the police report. "Ken, read this carefully. See if you see something that makes you think Mrs. Clark's death wasn't a suicide. Maybe you'll see something that I missed."

Gray took the report from Mohlar's trembling hands and thought, *He's still got his mind on that dream. He needs to lighten up.*

"I gotta tell you about the chick I met last night. Sam, she's just so fine. Renee's gotta be the most beautiful girl in the whole wide world. And guess what? She likes me."

"What happened to the girl you went out with a couple of days ago? You know, the night I met Clark."

"You mean Blanche. She is nice to me, but she's more interested in herself. Renee is interested in some stuff I'm interested in. She loves baseball, she loves to watch me play pool, and she loves me.

"After I finished talking to Clark, I picked up Renee at her hotel. We went to a local nightclub, had a few drinks, danced, and talked about baseball and pool until midnight. I took her back to her hotel room and we watched the movie *While You Were Sleeping*."

"I'm glad you had a good time with Renee. Tell me more about her at lunch. Would you read the police report now?"

As Gray read the police report, Mohlar carefully went over Gray's notes. Mohlar thought that Mrs. Clark was in very good spirits before her death for someone who was contemplating suicide.

After a while Gray said, "I see what you mean about the police report."

"What bothers you about it?" Mohlar asked.

Gray replied, "The report said that Mrs. Clark had her revolver in her right hand, but it also said that the bullet entered her head just above her left ear. It's almost impossible for her to shoot herself in the left side of the head with the gun in her right hand. And even if it was possible, it's not likely she'd shoot herself that way."

"That's exactly what I thought, Ken. Since there was no powder on her head, the wound was a non-contact wound. The distance the gun was from her head doesn't seem consistent with someone committing suicide."

"After talking to Miss Shaw, I think if Mrs. Clark committed suicide, she would've dressed up for it."

"She definitely would not have wanted to be found in her nightgown," Mohlar added.

After a few seconds, Gray said, "I doubt that she'd shoot herself in the head. Since the bullet hole would make her look ugly, she'd be more likely to take an overdose of sleeping pills or drink some poison."

Mohlar added, "It appears to me that she was in good spirits. She was planning a Caribbean cruise with her secretary. People who commit suicide don't plan trips."

"It seems to me that someone shot her and tried to make it look like suicide," Gray said. "I had the feeling that Marlo Shaw didn't really think that Krista wrote that note."

"I agree that she was murdered, but there's something else that puzzles me. The police report said that the bullet was fired from the gun found in her hand. That gun was registered in her name. How did the killer get the gun?"

"Maybe she got it out to protect herself when the killer came into her bedroom. Then the killer snatched it from her and shot her."

"Or maybe the killer knew where she kept the gun and got to it before Mrs. Clark," Mohlar added.

"But who would know where she kept the gun?"

"I don't know," Mohlar replied. "Let's review what we do know so far. Our client is the one person who has an unimpeachable alibi. He was at a retirement dinner when his wife was killed. The person he's certain killed his wife has the next best alibi. It appears that he was at a theater when the murder happened. It's possible he could've slipped out unnoticed, killed her, and returned in time for the final act of the play—"

"—he's sure acting guilty by running away, and no one knows where he is," Gray interrupted.

Mohlar continued, "Mrs. Berridge has a motive to kill Mrs. Clark and has no verifiable alibi. Miss Shaw has no alibi but has no apparent reason to kill her."

"Maybe she's still in love with Raymond Clark."

"It doesn't make sense that she would wait until after the Clarks had a separation to kill Mrs. Clark," Mohlar reasoned.

"When you talked to Clark, did you get the impression that he'll kill Flood when we find him?" Mohlar asked.

"It's hard to say. He told me that he wants him dead, but legally. As long as he thinks he'll stand trial for his wife's murder, I don't think he'll kill him."

"Ken, do you think I should tell Clark we'll take this case?"

"Yes. I want to figure out who killed Mrs. Clark, and I'd like to get paid for doing it."

"I'll tell him later today."

"Sam, maybe I should go to Syracuse this afternoon and see what I can find out from Olive Milby."

"Who is Olive Milby?"

"She's Dawn Berridge's grandmother and Richard Flood's mother. I want to see if her story is the same as Mrs. Berridge's. It took her way too long to travel from Syracuse to Rochester. I want to know when her grandmother says she left Syracuse. I also want to ask her where Flood is."

"If she's unwilling to tell you where Flood is, push her hard and maybe she'll talk. But, of course, she might not know where he is. If she doesn't tell you where he is, go to Pittsburgh and look for him there. I'll search for him in Buffalo. Before I go to Buffalo, I want to talk to Darren Aderman and William Goldberg. They may have information that will be helpful to us."

"Certainly Aderman believes he was cheated out of his inheritance and possibly was angry enough to kill his sister. We need to know why Mrs. Clark wanted to meet with her lawyer."

Looking at the clock, Mohlar said, "Ken, let's go to lunch."

SIX

Gray drove to the home of Olive Milby, noting its distance and driving time from the Clark house. He was still bothered by Dawn Berridge's statement that it took her four hours to drive from her grandmother's house to the Clark house. It took him less than two hours, and he wasn't even driving fast.

When Gray entered the living room of Olive Milby's house, the photographs and paintings on the walls impressed him. On one wall he saw framed photographs of New York Yankees—five players and one manager. The six photographs were arranged in the pattern of a triangle with the photograph of Joe DiMaggio on top. The one of Casey Stengel was signed.

Gray enjoyed talking with Mrs. Milby and thought of her as a very pleasant woman. "Mr. Gray, are you a baseball fan?" asked the short gray-haired woman.

"I follow the New York Yankees," he answered. "I check the paper daily to see how they're doing."

"I've been a Yankees fan for over sixty years. In fact, I went to Yankee Stadium and saw Joe DiMaggio play. He's my all-time favorite player. Do you know he holds the Major League record for the most consecutive games with at least one hit?"

"As I recall, in 1941 he hit safely in fifty-six consecutive games," Gray answered.

"You're right," she replied. "I remember well the day his hitting streak ended. While I was drying my mother's dishes, I was listening to the radio. When I heard the report that DiMaggio didn't get a hit in the game that day, his hitting streak ending, I was so upset that I threw the dishtowel on the floor. Unfortunately, there was a dish my parents got as a wedding present inside the towel. When my mother realized that her precious dish was broken, she got very angry with me.

"Do you know that the day after his consecutive game streak ended, he got a hit and started a sixteen game hitting streak?" Olive asked.

"Do you mean to say that he got at least one hit in seventy-two out of seventy-three consecutive games?"

"That's what I'm saying," she said.

"That is truly incredible," Gray said.

"Do you know who holds the longest hitting streak in the Pacific Coast Minor League?" she asked.

"I have a feeling the answer is Joe DiMaggio," Gray answered.

"You're right. In 1933 he had a sixty-one game streak with the San Francisco Seals."

Is she ever going to stop talking about baseball? Gray thought. *She's probably lonely and wants to seize the chance to talk to someone about baseball. I now know where Flood got his interest in baseball. Just be patient. I'll get a chance to change the subject...sometime.*

They continued talking about the Yankees for the next hour. Gray was fascinated by her knowledge of baseball and passion for the Yankees. Finally, she excused herself to the bathroom.

When she returned, and before she had a chance to say anything, Gray asked, "Do you know where Richard is?"

She answered in a worried tone, "No. I usually know where he is. However, a few days ago he called me and said that he had to leave Rochester. He thought it would be best not to tell me where he was going."

"Why did he want to leave Rochester?"

"I wish I knew the answer to that question," she replied with a sigh. "I wonder if he's in some sort of trouble."

Her mind wondered. *You'd think when they get older, you wouldn't worry so much, but I guess I worry more now than ever before,* she thought.

"Where does he usually go when he goes on a vacation?" Gray asked, but Olive didn't answer. Gray saw she was deep in thought.

"Mrs. Milby, uh, Mrs. Milby," Gray said with a raised voice.

"Yes," she said as she brought her mind back to the discussion.

"Where does Richard usually go when he goes on a vacation?"

"He usually goes to Buffalo. Sometimes he goes to Pittsburgh."

"Do you have any relatives in Buffalo or Pittsburgh?"

"No," she answered with sharpness in her voice. "Why are you asking me all these questions?"

"Richard's former boss, Krista Clark, recently died, and Richard can help us answer some questions about her death."

"My granddaughter also worked for Mrs. Clark. Maybe she could help you."

"I've already talked to her, but I also want to talk to your son. She said that she visited you last Saturday. Do you remember what time she left you?"

"She left around seven o'clock, maybe a little later. She is such a dear girl. She loves to come and visit me, and we have such good times together."

Gray could see that she was ready to get off the subject again. Trying to bring her back to the point of his visit, he asked, "And Richard, does he see you much?"

"He keeps in touch pretty well. Just last week he sent me a letter and enclosed eight one hundred-dollar bills. That's the first time he ever did that. He's often helped me, but never with money. In fact, it's kind of strange, isn't it? He lost his job and he sent me money," she mused with a puzzled look on her face. *I do wish I would hear from him,* she thought.

"Do you remember the exact day you got the letter from Richard?" Gray looked intently at her and thought, *Oh dear, I've lost her again.*

He said, while shaking her arm, "Mrs. Milby." When her eyes

focused on him, he repeated, "Do you remember the exact day you got the letter from Richard?"

Olive was silent for a few seconds before answering. "I got the letter Saturday, March 26."

Gray wrote himself a note that Mrs. Milby received money from Flood on the same day Krista Clark died.

"Did he say why he sent you the money?"

"He wrote that he had some extra money and thought maybe I could use it. He knows that I live on a very tight budget, and I'm behind in paying some of my bills."

"If you find out where Richard is, would you let me know?" Gray asked as he handed her his business card.

"I'll ask Richard if he cares if anyone knows where he is. If he doesn't care, I'll tell you."

Gray thanked Olive for giving him so much time. He then departed for Pittsburgh.

———

While Gray was in Syracuse, Mohlar went to William Goldberg's house. It was a large, old, handsome red brick house with two big bay windows in front. In back of the house, rows of brown cornstalks were visible, the remains of last year's harvest.

Mrs. Goldberg showed Mohlar to the library, where her husband was sitting at his desk taking notes while referring to a law book. He was approximately forty-five years old with aggressive brown eyes behind black-rimmed glasses that rested on a long, thin nose. He took off his glasses and laid them on the desk. The library was a clean room with attractive paintings of the ocean shore on the walls and a meticulous order among its books.

"My name is Sam Mohlar," he said slowly as he admired the books on the shelves.

William Goldberg looked puzzled and said, "So what? What are you doing here?"

"I've been asked to investigate the death of Krista Clark. I've been told that Mrs. Clark had an appointment to see you the Monday following her death."

"That's correct," Goldberg replied.

"What did she want to see you about? Was it concerning personal or business affairs?"

"I can't tell you. Conversations between lawyers and clients are confidential."

"Mr. Goldberg, I want you to understand the seriousness of what I'm requesting of you. I'm sure Mrs. Clark was murdered. The information you're withholding from me could help me determine who killed her. Don't you want the person who killed Mrs. Clark punished?"

"I thought Mrs. Clark's death was ruled a suicide."

"Mrs. Clark's death looked like a suicide, but my partner and I have discovered evidence that shows her death was a homicide."

"Show me this evidence."

Mohlar grabbed a piece of paper out of his pocket and gave it to Goldberg. "Here's a copy of the police report. I noted and commented on the parts that led me to think Clark was murdered."

Goldberg picked up his glasses and set them on his nose. After taking a few minutes to read the report, he leaned forward in his chair, looked at Mohlar with eyes as hard as the lenses over them, and said, "Actually, it's irrelevant to me how she died. I can't tell you anything about why Mrs. Clark wanted to see me last Monday."

"How large is the company that Mr. Clark inherited when Mrs. Clark died?"

Goldberg's eyes softened and he answered, "It's one of the largest plastics companies in the country."

"Maybe you can answer this question: Why did Darren Aderman think he was cheated out of his inheritance?"

"Darren was the only child of Gary and Joyce Aderman. When Darren was two years old, Joyce died in an automobile accident. Six months later Gary married Minerva Perdue. When Darren was four years old, Gary and Minerva had their only child, Krista. By that time Gary was a very successful businessman. Actually, he was a pioneer in the plastic industry. Just before Krista was born, Gary and Minerva hired my father to handle their legal affairs. When Krista was sixteen, Gary died of a heart attack. He left his entire fortune and control of his business to his wife, Minerva. Darren thought that as the oldest child he should've received some of the inheritance. He accused my father of advising Gary to leave the entire inheritance to Minerva. He has hated my father ever since his father died. Then just four months ago, Minerva died. He thought he'd receive about half of Minerva Aderman's fortune. However, she left him a very small percent of her fortune. Krista received almost all of her fortune."

Goldberg took his glasses off and shook them for emphasis, as he said, "Darren accused me of manipulating things so that he was left out of the inheritance. He was hurt and angry, but there was nothing he could do."

"Was Darren angry at his sister because she got most of the inheritance?"

"He was very angry at her because he thought that she and I conspired to cheat him out of a fortune."

"Do you think he was angry enough to kill his sister?"

"Maybe...well...I don't know. He really didn't need his stepmother's money. He himself is a rich man."

Mohlar thanked him for his help and gave him his business card as he left.

———

Mohlar went to see Raymond Clark. As he was traveling, he was pondering Goldberg's answer to his last question. Usually when a person is asked whether someone could kill a close relative, the answer is an emphatic "no," but Goldberg's immediate response was that Aderman had possibly killed his sister. The response was unusual but possibly unimportant.

Mohlar found Clark in his hotel room. The detective said, "Gray and I have decided to help you find Flood."

"Good," replied Clark. "I wrote a contract and made a copy of it for us to sign."

When Mohlar saw the contract, he was surprised that it was not typed but handwritten with each letter carefully printed. After he read the document, Mohlar said, "This looks fine. However, I noticed that you make some of your letters in an unusual way."

Ignoring Mohlar's comments about his handwriting, Clark said, "Please sign the original and the copy on the dotted line and I will also."

After signing the contract, Mohlar asked, "Do you want me to give you e-mail reports when we make progress?"

"No, I tend to stay away from computers. Give me an oral report everyday whether or not you make any progress. If you contact Flood, I expect you to call me immediately."

"Gray and I think that Flood is either in Buffalo or Pittsburgh. We'll start our search for him in those cities tomorrow."

————

Mohlar left to see Darren Aderman, who lived on the east side of Rochester. His mansion was set in the middle of six acres of land, which were enclosed with a white fence. Mohlar squinted his eyes as he walked toward the house because the gold doorknocker and handle gleamed in the afternoon sun.

The butler opened the door after Mohlar knocked. "What name shall I say?" the butler asked.

"Samuel Mohlar, Raymond Clark's friend."

After a few minutes, the butler returned. He said, "Follow me."

He led Mohlar down a hallway and to the door of the music room. When the butler opened the door, a gray-haired man of medium height and build approached Mohlar. He was very well-dressed with a large diamond in his tie. "My name is Darren Aderman."

When he stretched out his hand to shake Mohlar's, Mohlar noticed a four-baguette diamond ring on his ring finger. His hands were small, soft, and well-cared for. The diamonds on his hand and tie twinkled in the light. Aderman invited Mohlar in and said, "The name Samuel Mohlar means nothing to me. Would you tell me why you want to see me?"

"I'm investigating the death of your sister. Your brother-in-law believes she was murdered. He thinks that Richard Flood killed her. What do you think?"

As they both sat down, Aderman said, "I don't really know him well enough to say one way or the other. I'll call my wife in here. She may remember things about Flood that I can't remember."

"Hattie, come in here!" Aderman yelled.

Soon a shapely woman wearing a red sweater and black slacks entered the room. Mohlar guessed she was about forty. *Her facial beauty is about seven years past its best year*, he thought. "Mr. Mohlar, this is my wife, Hattie."

"Do you know where I might find Richard Flood?" Mohlar inquired.

"No," Hattie answered.

"What do you know about Flood? Was he a violent man?" Mohlar asked as he studied her face.

"I really don't know," Hattie replied.

Turning back to Darren, he said, "Some people have said that your relationship with your sister was strained. Do you agree with them?"

Aderman shifted uncomfortably in his chair as he answered, "Yes. My sister and her Jewish lawyer friend, Goldberg, cheated me out of my family's fortune. I'll never forgive them for that. Besides, she never liked Hattie. She treated her like a leper. Fifteen years ago she didn't even attend our wedding. As far as I'm concerned, if she doesn't like Hattie, she doesn't like me."

Mohlar looked at him with probing eyes, trying to decide if he was hiding something, and asked, "Why do you think Goldberg had anything to do with you being excluded from obtaining an inheritance? He was merely the lawyer that made out the papers expressing the wishes of your mother."

"All Jews are the same. They're after everything they can get. Goldberg knew that if I gained control of my family's company, he'd be out as the lawyer for the business. Goldberg's father knew how I felt about Jews, and that's why he convinced my father to exclude me from his will and leave everything to my mother. As his only son and oldest child, I should've been given control of the business."

"Would you tell me how long you've known Raymond Clark, and what you and Raymond do in the plastic factory?"

"I've known Raymond Clark for about thirty years. We played on the same basketball team in college. During our college years, he dated my sister off and on. Raymond Clark, Marlo Shaw, my sister, and I graduated together. My sister made sure Raymond got a job in our family business. Not long after he got the job, they broke up. She knew he was only after her money. But she loved him and after a few months they started dating again. About two years after we graduated from college, Krista and Raymond were married.

"Ever since I graduated from college, I've managed the Research and Development Department of the company. Raymond has always been in charge of the Accounting Department. He periodically takes inventories of our supplies and products. When Krista died, her will made Raymond the CEO of the company."

"Are you angry that Mr. Clark is the CEO of the company?" Mohlar asked.

Aderman looked at him with cold eyes and answered, "Of course I am. My father founded and built this company into an industrial power. Now someone who isn't even blood related to my father is my boss. The company should be mine, and it would be mine if it weren't for those fast talking, deceiving lawyers—the Goldbergs."

Mohlar was not surprised at his candor; he, too, would be upset. "I know Flood likes to gamble. Can you tell me anything else about him, even if it seems insignificant?" Mohlar asked.

"One time when we were at the Clark house visiting Darren's mother, Flood was there with his girlfriend, his daughter, and Marlo Shaw. He introduced us to his girlfriend, but I don't remember her name. Anyway, she asked Flood if he'd go to church with her that night. I was surprised that he got so upset with her for asking a question. He said that he had gone to church with her the night before and said something like, 'Quit pushing me about church.' I remember the exact words of her response. She said, 'It's okay if you don't go to church, but it's not okay if you reject God.'"

"Could you try to remember her name?" Mohlar asked.

"Her name was Cheryl or Karen or something like that," Darren said.

"Could her name be Carol?" Mohlar asked.

"Yes, that's it," Darren said. "But I don't remember her last name."

"Wilson?" Mohlar asked.

"I said I don't remember her last name," Darren said in an irritated tone.

"Flood came to our house once to pick up a DVD for Darren's mother," Hattie said in a quivering voice. "He became angry when Darren had trouble finding it. He said we should've found it before he arrived. Darren soon found it. It seems to me that Flood isn't very patient."

"There's something I don't understand. Why do you have a key to the Clark house?" Mohlar asked while looking directly at Darren.

"When my mother needed almost constant care, she went to live with my sister. The Clarks wanted me to feel as though I could stop in to be with her at anytime, especially while they were not at home."

"Why didn't you return the key after Mrs. Aderman died?"

Darren gritted his teeth, clenched his fists, and said, "I forgot to give it back. I didn't kill my sister if that is what you're hinting."

"Where were you last Saturday night?"

As Darren's face became red, he said, "You're not the police. I don't have to answer your questions."

"Do you have something to hide, Aderman?"

Darren pounded the table with his fist and yelled, "No. Get out of my house!"

Mohlar turned and stalked rigidly from the house. *Is this man capable of murder?* he asked himself. He returned home and prepared to leave for Buffalo the next day.

SEVEN

Mohlar rented a large furnished two–bedroom apartment on the west side of Buffalo. He had one large window in the apartment, which overlooked a highway frequently used by truckers. The traffic noise was always loud, but the noise didn't bother him.

Gray rented a small one-bedroom apartment in a suburb of Pittsburgh, which had two small windows. The neighborhood was so quiet that the birds startled him when they began singing near his windows.

Day after day for four months Mohlar and Gray searched for Flood. They showed photos of Flood to thousands of people, including hotel clerks, bartenders, waitresses, taxi drivers, gas station attendants, and barbers. They made inquiries at apartment houses and utility companies. They visited many racetracks, casinos, and bingo halls. They went to every sports card show they could find. They played many games of poker hoping to find Flood there.

One hot July Saturday, Mohlar wanted to see if Flood was at a poker game in the back of Johnson's Poolroom. He was told that the poolroom was near the bus station on Pascal Street. After he parked his car, he walked up and down Pascal Street, but he couldn't find Johnson's Poolroom.

He saw an old man handing out leaflets on Pascal. As Mohlar approached him, the old man gave him a leaflet and asked, "Do you know Jesus Christ?"

"I know who He is, but I'm not a believer," Mohlar answered

while putting the leaflet into his pocket. "Do you know where Johnson's Poolroom is?"

"Johnson's recently changed ownership. Now it's called Smith's."

Mohlar found Smith's and walked in. At Smith's, ten men were playing pool at six tables with no more than two players at one table. He asked a man playing by himself where he could find the poker game. The man, without saying a word, pointed to the back of the room.

The door to the back room was open, so Mohlar walked in. Four men were sitting around a circular table playing cards, but Flood was not there. At first no one paid attention to him—maybe they didn't know he was there. Mohlar noticed that the betting limit was five dollars, and usually the bets didn't go that high.

Mohlar didn't like gambling. Every gambler loses sometimes— and he hated to lose. But he didn't like winning either. When he won, he felt like he was stealing other people's money. He looked at gambling as an unpleasant part of his current job.

Mohlar was pleased to see they were playing blackjack. He was a good blackjack player because he counted cards. He ignored the sevens, eights, and nines, but made a mental note of every other card that was played. By doing this, he knew when the deck was heavy in high-point cards or when it was heavy in low-point cards.

As Mohlar listened to the conversation of the four men, he learned their names. While he was waiting to get into the game, he evaluated the skill level of the four men at the table.

Lynn Babcock, the oldest of the four players, was always staring at the table. Anyone that tense at a game of blackjack had to be counting cards. Although he almost always played the percentages, he didn't on the last hand. He had a total of nine on his first two cards and the dealer's up-card was a three, but he didn't double his bet. If he had done that, he would have won twice as much money. *Maybe he played cautiously because he can't afford to lose any money,* Mohlar thought. *This may work to my advantage if I were to get into the game.*

The man closest to Mohlar, sitting next to Babcock, was a middle-aged man named Ed Downs. He had one blue eye and one brown eye. Mohlar had never seen anyone with different-colored eyes. Downs, the richest of the four players, played blackjack based more on hunches and emotions than odds. Mohlar sensed that Downs would lose his temper if he had a run of bad luck.

The man next to Downs was Lee Thompson. He was a middle-aged man who was an experienced blackjack player. Although he appeared to be relaxed, Mohlar could tell he was counting cards because he regularly adjusted the height of one of his stacks of chips. Thompson calculated the odds of winning and played accordingly.

The man farthest from Mohlar and next to Thompson was a young man named Paul Himes. He was wearing a sport coat that bulged in such a way that made Mohlar wonder what he was hiding. Mohlar noticed that he often played foolishly. In the last game Mohlar didn't understand why he continued taking cards. He had a total of seventeen and the dealer's up-card was a three. Himes went bust when he asked for another card.

Mohlar liked his chances of winning if he could get into the game. By playing the percentages, he anticipated beating Himes and Downs. Depending on luck, he may or may not end up winning against Thompson and Babcock.

Mohlar waited patiently to be invited into the game. He thought, *Thompson and Babcock are avid card players. Downs and Himes are avid sports card collectors. If Flood is in Buffalo, there's a good chance someone here has seen him. I've got to get into this game and talk to them.*

Fifteen minutes later, Babcock finally said, "Want to join the game? But if you join us, I'll still be the dealer until the next blackjack."

"I've got money and I want to play," the detective said while pulling a chair up to the table between Babcock and Downs. The chair was well-padded and open-backed.

Mohlar won the first game with three cards totaling twenty-one. He won the second game with a king and ten—a total of twenty.

He thought, *This is too easy. They may be hustling me. I'm not go-*

ing to play very long if these guys are cheating. On the other hand, I knew the deck was heavy in high-count cards, so it's not surprising I was dealt these five cards.

Mohlar often won at card games such as blackjack and poker. He knew how to play the odds—most mathematicians do.

Yet odds are meaningless when people cheat. At first hustlers deal cards so their patsy wins. After a while, the patsy starts losing. When the patsy counts his money at the end of the game, he finds that he has lost hundreds of dollars. So everyone goes home happy, except the patsy.

Mohlar watched the men carefully, especially the dealer, to see if he could spot any cheating. He knew how to detect communication between players through their table talk. He watched to see if players were getting cards from their shirts or other players. After a few games, he knew these men were playing honestly.

During the next hour, Mohlar dealt most of the time. Two games ago, Babcock got a blackjack and had become the new dealer. During that time Downs had a run of bad luck and had become very grumpy.

While Babcock was pouring everyone a drink, Mohlar pulled a picture out of his pocket. He said, "I'm looking for a man who likes to gamble. Here's a picture of him. Have you seen him?"

"What's his name?" Thompson asked.

"Richard Flood," Mohlar answered.

Each man said that he had not seen Flood.

"There's a poker game on Riemann Street tomorrow morning," Babcock said. "Mohlar, do you think you'll be there?"

"Maybe," Mohlar answered.

Babcock dealt each man their first card, facedown, on the table. Mohlar looked at his card, a six, and made the minimum bet. After everyone placed his bet, Babcock dealt each man his face-up card. Mohlar's second card was a king, giving him a total of sixteen. Babcock's up-card was a seven.

Mohlar thought, *At this point in the game, there are the same number of low cards as high cards in the deck. If I take another card, the odds are eight to five of breaking twenty-one. I'll break if I get a card different from an ace or two through five. If I stand on these two cards, Babcock will probably beat me.* "Hit me," Mohlar whispered.

Babcock tossed Mohlar a card that landed face up in front of Mohlar's king. It was an ace. Although Mohlar wanted to be closer to twenty-one, he said, "I'll stand."

Downs looked with vicious eyes at Mohlar's ace. After a few seconds, Downs said, "Hit me." Babcock flipped him a five, which landed next to his exposed four. After Downs hesitated for a second, he said, "Hit me." He pounded the table with his fist as he watched a jack land in front of him. "I went bust," he said while turning over his down-card, a six.

"If you had not drawn a card, Mohlar, I would've won. That ace would've given me twenty-one," Downs angrily told Mohlar.

"Calm down," Mohlar said in response to Down's outburst of anger. "Maybe you'll be luckier next game."

"I'd like to know what your down-card is. If you played stupid by taking an extra card, I'll knock those pretty teeth of yours down your throat," Downs threatened.

Mohlar thought, *Played stupid! Look who's saying that to me. He's played against the percentages often and he just did it again. Why didn't he double his bet when his first two cards totaled ten and the dealer's up-card was a seven? I'd like to give that guy a right hook to the head.*

"If you try messing with me, I'll change those two eyes of yours to the same color—both red," Mohlar responded. As Himes put his hand inside his sport coat, Downs moved his head from side to side. Himes then put his hands into the pockets of his slacks.

"Calm down, boys," Babcock said. "Let's play cards."

After Thompson and Himes went bust, everyone knew that Babcock would collect all the bets if he could beat Mohlar. Babcock carefully looked at Mohlar's up-cards. While turning over his down-card, a queen, he said, "I'll stand."

Mohlar turned over his down-card and said, "I lose because we both have seventeen." Mohlar turned his head toward Downs and said to him, "Do you still want to mess with me?"

"Deal the cards," Downs said to Babcock, ignoring Mohlar's comment.

Babcock said, "Let's take a break for a few minutes. I'd like to visit the men's room."

"This has been a bad day for me," Downs said. "I'm overdue to get a blackjack."

Mohlar, in an attempt to smooth things over between Downs and himself, said, "Your luck is bound to change. You've been playing smart, but you've been unlucky."

Mohlar glanced at Thompson and saw him crack a smile. He knew Mohlar had just told Downs a white lie.

A few minutes later Babcock returned. He walked toward Mohlar and stopped beside him. When no one was looking his way, he slipped Mohlar a note. Mohlar put the note into his pocket and went to the restroom.

He opened up Babcock's note and read, "Be careful of Downs. He's a hothead, and he has a friend—Himes."

When Mohlar returned, everyone was sitting at the table. Mohlar sat between Babcock and Downs.

Downs got a blackjack on the next deal, giving him the privilege of being the next dealer. Mohlar lost again, his third consecutive loss, but he was still over fifty dollars ahead.

"I'll cash in my chips now. It was nice playing cards with you guys," the detective said.

"I don't think so, Mohlar. You can't quit while I'm dealing. You've got to give me a chance to win back some of my money."

Downs nodded to someone standing behind Mohlar. *Himes must be behind me because he is no longer at the table*, Mohlar thought. Immediately Mohlar felt something hard pressing on the spine of his lower back.

"I think Downs is right. It's rude to quit while you're ahead. This gun you feel says that you'll quit when we say we're done."

Mohlar turned his head. Himes was close behind him, smiling broadly as if he were wishing for a chance to pull the trigger of the gun.

Suddenly, Mohlar lunged backwards with all his strength. His momentum pushed the crossbar of the back of the chair so fast that it hit the gun and pulled it from Himes's hand before he could pull the trigger.

Mohlar went head-over-heels onto the floor, landing close to Himes and the gun. When Himes went to pick up the gun, Mohlar drove his right fist against Himes's chin. Mohlar followed with a vicious left hook, landing on the right side of Himes's head. Dazed, Himes dropped the gun and he fell to the floor.

Downs grabbed Mohlar from behind. Mohlar pushed back his two arms and his elbows hit Downs in the ribs. Downs let go of Mohlar and bent over in pain. Mohlar grabbed the gun.

Mohlar pointed the gun at Downs and yelled, "Everybody, put your hands up." The four men quickly obeyed Mohlar's command.

"Himes, I think you misunderstood the gun. Actually, the gun said I can leave anytime I want. I'm cashing in my chips now and leaving. You're to stay in this room until I'm out of the Poolroom."

When Mohlar grabbed his money and left the room, he put the gun in his pocket because he didn't want to alarm the men playing pool. He dropped the gun immediately after leaving Smith's.

Mohlar was irritated that he allowed Himes to put a gun against his back. Sweat had formed on his face and some of it was dripping on his shirt. As he walked to his car, he recalled that Babcock said there was a poker game tomorrow on Riemann Street. Maybe Flood would be at that game, but probably not.

Mohlar was frustrated and discouraged. Daily Gray would call Mohlar and tell him that he had not found Flood. Then Mohlar would call Clark and tell him that he had not found Flood either.

On this hot Saturday in July, Mohlar ended his report to Clark by saying, "I don't know how long you want to fund this search. If Flood is in Buffalo or Pittsburgh, I think he has changed his name. I'll understand if you want to stop."

"Don't be discouraged," Clark said. "I want you to find Flood, and I don't care how long it takes."

"As long as you're willing to pay us, we'll keep looking."

Mohlar had never been more discouraged in his life. After he hung up the telephone, he reached into his pocket and pulled out the leaflet the old man on Pascal Street had given him. He saw in large print at the top of the leaflet *What to Read in Times of Need*. He looked down the list of needs and noticed the heading *Discouragement*. Then he read:

> Trust in the LORD with all your heart and lean not on your own understanding; in all ways acknowledge him, and he will make your paths straight.
>
> Proverbs 3:5–6

> Ask and it will be given you; seek and you will find; knock and the door will be opened to you. For everyone who asks receives; he who seeks finds; and to him who knocks, the door will be opened.
>
> Matthew 7:7–8

After reading these words from the Bible, Mohlar thought, *Maybe I should ask God to help me find Flood. It wouldn't hurt; maybe it would even help. I haven't anything to lose. But why would God help me?* Mohlar asked himself as he sat up with his head in his hands. *I rarely think about Him. I haven't prayed to Him since I was a kid. And I'm such a wretched person. The thoughts I have when I see attractive women must be disgusting to Him.*

Mohlar stood up and paced the room, wringing his hands. *I'll never find Flood. He may not even be in Buffalo or Pittsburgh. In fact, he may have left the country. If I'm ever going to find Flood, I'll need God's help.*

Mohlar dropped to his knees, bowed his head, and said, "Oh, God, I'm sorry I haven't talked to you in a long time. You know how long I've searched for this guy, Flood. I'm asking you to help me find him." At that time, he didn't realize that the events of the next day would change his life.

EIGHT

The next morning Mohlar decided to eat breakfast at a café two blocks east of his apartment. He said to a smiling waitress, "I'd like three eggs covered with mushrooms, four slices of toast, and orange juice."

"It sounds like you want Eggs à la Reine. That's poached eggs covered with sautéed mushrooms and a hot cheese sauce. Is that what you want?"

"Sounds great," Mohlar responded.

Soon his breakfast came and his eggs were delicious. While he was eating his eggs, an average sized, gray-haired man dressed in a suit walked up to him and said, "May I join you for a few minutes?"

Mohlar rolled his eyes and answered, "Go ahead."

"My name is Bob Raze."

"You can call me Sam," Mohlar replied.

"How are things going with you, Sam?"

"I doubt that you'd be interested in my problems."

"I'm interested," Raze responded. "Each Sunday morning I go to the neighborhood restaurants. I ask people in the restaurants if they're having problems. Hopefully, I can help them."

"I doubt you can help me, but I'll give you a chance," the detective said as he pulled two pictures out of his pocket. "Have you ever seen this man?"

Raze took the pictures and examined them closely. He shook his head and said, "I haven't seen him."

"I'm a private investigator," Mohlar said. "I've been hired to find the man in those pictures. I've been looking for him for almost four months, but haven't been able to find him."

"When I have problems in my life, I've always found that it helps to go to church," Raze said. "Why don't you go to church with me today? You'll feel better after spending a couple of hours in church."

Mohlar thought, *This man sure is pushy. Sam, try to respond politely.* "Thanks for the invitation, but I don't think going to church will help me. Besides, I was going to play some poker with some men this morning. The man in the pictures might be at the poker game. It was nice meeting you, Mr. Raze."

After Raze left the cafe, Mohlar finished his breakfast. He left a generous tip because the waitress suggested a delicious recipe for eggs.

As Mohlar was walking toward his car, he thought, *Flood probably won't be at that poker game because he wasn't there last week. Maybe I should see if it would help me to go to church today. I wish I'd have accepted Raze's invitation. I'll just drive around and find a church.*

After driving around for a while, he came to a large church in a suburb of Buffalo. The building was unique in appearance. The front was modern looking with a large cross and large clear windows. The rest of the building appeared to have been built more than one hundred years before. The old part of the church had magnificent stained glass windows.

While walking toward the church, Mohlar heard the pleasant tones of a pipe organ. The wonderful music encouraged him to go inside.

At first he felt awkward when he went in the unusual building because he had not attended church in many years. However, as time went on, he felt better. The people of the church had a way of making him feel comfortable.

A young man wearing new blue jeans and a faded red shirt asked, "Would you like to go downstairs with me to meet some people before the worship service starts? The women of the church are serving donuts, coffee, tea, and orange juice."

"No thanks. I'll wait in the sanctuary for the church service to start."

Then an elderly man wearing a dark suit and striped tie asked, "Do you live around here?"

"I'm from Rochester, but now I live and work in Buffalo."

"Is this the first time you've come to this church?" the elderly man asked.

Mohlar answered as tension left his face, "Yes."

"Wait here a minute," the man said. When he returned, he handed Mohlar a visitor's packet welcoming him to the church.

After saying good-bye to the elderly man, Mohlar entered the sanctuary and sat in a pew toward the front. Five minutes after he sat down, the pastor said, "Some of you may be going through a difficult time. Jesus can help you no matter what problems you have.

"Please turn to hymn number fifty-three, written by Tommy Dorsey. He was not the famous bandleader, but was called 'The Father of Gospel Music.' Please sing with me 'Precious Lord, Take My Hand' and believe the words in this song."

Mohlar wanted to believe the message of the song, but it just didn't make sense to him. He reasoned that if everyone brought their problems to God, He couldn't deal with all of them. God would pay attention to the big problems of the day, like famine and war, instead of helping him find a missing person.

After finishing the Dorsey hymn, the pastor said, "Maybe you're thinking God isn't powerful enough to handle your problems. Don't you think the One who created this world and everything in it is powerful enough to handle your problems?

"Think about that question while we sing hymn number 127, 'This is My Father's World.' Malbie Babcock, who lived just twenty miles from here in Lockport, New York, wrote this hymn. Please stand to sing it."

After they finished this hymn, the pastor said, "You may be

seated. Maybe you believe God is powerful enough to fix your problems, but why would He bother with your problems when He has so many big problems to deal with in the universe? Well, the Bible says that even the hairs of your head are numbered. It says He cares when a sparrow falls. God cares about what He has created. Think about that as we sing hymn number 422, 'His Eye is on the Sparrow.'"

Is this guy reading my mind or what? Mohlar thought as he sang this hymn. *Okay, God loves the birds and He counts my hairs. If He's counted my hairs, He must know what I've done, and I've done some pretty terrible things. It was stupid of me to ask God for help last night. What am I doing here anyway?*

After a while, the pastor said, "Please turn in your Bibles to Romans 6:23." After a moment, he read, "For the wages of sin is death, but the gift of God is eternal life in Christ Jesus our Lord."

The pastor continued, "Let's consider what this verse is saying. When you receive wages for work, you get paid for what you do. For example, if you tell a neighbor boy you'll pay him twenty dollars for mowing the lawn, the boy will expect that payment when he finishes the job. So a wage is a payment the recipient deserves.

"Recall last week I defined sin as a breaking of a law or a commandment of God. The Bible says that it doesn't matter if we break this law intentionally or unintentionally, it is still a sin. Recall last week I showed from the Bible that we are all sinners.

"Perhaps some of you have thought you're going to heaven because you haven't done really bad things, like murder or adultery. Jesus said that if you're angry with someone, it's as though you've committed murder. He also said that if you look lustfully at a woman, you've committed adultery with her in your heart. According to the Bible, you can sin by having thoughts that are against God's law.

"So this verse says that the payment for sin that we deserve is death. The death spoken about isn't a physical death, but a spiritual death.

"What will the spiritual death be like? Let's read Luke 16:19–

31 to answer this question. This is found on page 876 in the pew Bible."

Mohlar picked up a Bible from the back of the pew in front of him and turned to where the pastor was reading. He saw the following:

> There was a rich man who was dressed in purple and fine linen and lived in luxury every day. At his gate was laid a beggar named Lazarus, covered with sores and longing to eat what fell from the rich man's table. Even the dogs came and licked his sores. The time came when the beggar died and the angels carried him to Abraham's side. The rich man also died and was buried. In hell, where he was in torment, he looked up and saw Abraham far away, with Lazarus by his side. So he called to him, "Father Abraham, have pity on me and send Lazarus to dip the tip of his finger in water and cool my tongue, because I am in agony in this fire." But Abraham replied, "Son, remember that in your lifetime you received your good things, while Lazarus received bad things, but now he is comforted here and you are in agony. And besides all this, between us and you a great chasm has been fixed, so that those who want to go from here to you cannot, nor can anyone cross over from there to us."
>
> He answered, "Then I beg you, father, send Lazarus to my father's house, for I have five brothers. Let him warn them, so that they will not also come to this place of torment." Abraham replied, "They have Moses and the Prophets; let them listen to them."
>
> "No, father Abraham," he said, "but if someone from the dead goes to them, they will repent." He said to him, "If they do not listen to Moses and the Prophets, they will not be convinced even if someone rises from the dead."

The pastor continued, "So anyone who endures the spiritual death will spend an eternity away from God, where he'll be in torment and agony."

Mohlar was struck with fear as he listened to the pastor. This fear was similar to the fear he had in his nightmares. He could feel his body shaking and sweat on his forehead. The pastor had described the scene in his nightmares, and Mohlar realized he was heading there. He wondered how he could escape going to the place where the rich man was.

After the pastor paused for a few seconds, he said, "Recall the Bible said, 'The gift of God is eternal life in Christ Jesus our Lord.' Suppose someone has something for you. What must happen in order for that thing to be a gift? First, you must accept the thing that is offered by taking it; otherwise, the thing isn't yours. Second, you must not pay for it. If you pay for it, it's not a gift, but rather something you've earned.

"So every sinner, who is every person, deserves a spiritual death. This death can be avoided by accepting the gift of eternal life offered by God.

"Who paid for the gift? Jesus paid the price when he was hung to die upon a wooden cross. He was punished for our sins. The verse in Romans I read to you said that we are offered a gift, and that gift is eternal life. The Bible says there's only one way to God, the Father, and that is through his Son, Jesus.

"So the choice is yours. You can take the wages of your sin and endure a spiritual death, or you can accept the gift of eternal life, and after your physical death you will escape a spiritual death. I invite you right now to ask God to forgive you of your sins. Tell Him that you want to accept his gift of eternal life so that from this moment on you may start living forever with God."

As soon as the pastor finished speaking, Mohlar said to himself, *Lord Jesus, I know I'm a sinner. I know that when I look lustfully at attractive women, I sin against you, Lord. Please forgive me of my sins. Help me not to sin anymore. I accept this free gift from you of eternal life.*

At that moment Mohlar could not believe the tremendous feeling of relief that overcame him. He experienced a peace within him that he never had before. He felt like a new person.

As Mohlar was leaving the church, he bumped into a large man who twisted him around. He clearly saw another man who was heading toward the door. He was slightly taller than average. He had a thin nose, high cheekbones, a gray mustache, and blue eyes. He matched perfectly the appearance of the man in the two pictures in his pocket—there was no mistake about it. Flood was about to walk out of the church.

Since the church was crowded that day, many people stood between them, which prevented him from reaching Flood. Mohlar felt like pushing people out of the way, but he thought that would be an inappropriate action for someone in church. When he finally made his way through the crowd, he ran to the parking lot. He looked around and saw Flood get into his car. As Flood drove off, Mohlar read the license plate number. Since he didn't have any paper on him, he wrote the number on his hand.

He went back into the church and asked everyone he saw if they knew Flood. No one knew him. He checked the guest register, but no one had signed it that day.

After Mohlar left the church, he called Gray. "Ken, guess who I saw in church today?"

"Oh, how 'bout the Pope?" Gray replied.

"No, I saw Flood. Get to Buffalo as soon as you can because tomorrow we are going to track him down."

Mohlar was eager to call Clark so he could give him some good news for a change, yet Mohlar was even more anxious to see his friend Ken and tell him about what he had heard in church that morning.

NINE

When Gray arrived at Mohlar's apartment at eight in the evening, he said, "Who would've thought you'd find Flood in a church? It sure looks like this is our lucky day. Whatever made you look in a church of all places?"

"Luck had nothing to do with it. Last night I asked God to help us find Flood. I believe God guided me to that church today so I'd find Flood."

Mohlar told Gray what he had heard in church. He finished by suggesting to Gray that he, too, believe in Jesus Christ.

Gray said, "I think Christians are a bunch of hypocrites. When I was young, there was a man in my church who didn't keep himself clean. Most people in the church shunned him. These people were friendly to everyone in the church except the unclean man. They told the priest they didn't want this unclean man coming to the church; so the priest told that man he would not be allowed to attend church services until he got clean. My father asked the priest to change his decision, but the priest didn't change his mind. If Christians say they love everybody, they should act lovingly to everybody. If Christians exclude people from church services, I don't want any part of Christianity."

"People make mistakes," Mohlar said. "I learned today that we are all sinners and deserve to die. We can avoid this death and live forever by believing in Jesus."

Gray said, "I don't have enough faith to believe. It's nice that you do, but don't push me to believe as you do."

Mohlar changed the subject by saying, "Do you remember telling me about the conversation you had with Mrs. Milby? It just doesn't make sense to me that Flood would send his mother eight hundred dollars about a week after he was fired from his job, especially since he had not been in the habit of sending her money."

"Maybe Flood got lucky playing cards or playing the horses," Gray replied.

Then Mohlar said, "Would you go to the Department of Motor Vehicles tomorrow morning? Find out the name and address of the person who owns the car with the license plate number I wrote on my hand earlier today. While I've been looking for Flood in Buffalo, I found a man who has an extensive baseball card collection. He has some old rare cards that I might be able to use as bait for Flood. While you're at the Department of Motor Vehicles, I'll see if I can buy some cards from him."

Gray nodded his head in agreement and said, "Sam, yesterday I heard a math puzzle that stumped me. The person who told me the puzzle said that he knows of only one person, besides himself, who has solved it."

"I love solving math puzzles, especially challenging ones."

"Suppose you're blindfolded and someone lays a deck of fifty-two playing cards on a table in front of you, where ten are face up and the rest are face down. How would you move the cards so that the same number of cards are face up on your left side as on your right side?"

"Easy puzzle to solve," Mohlar said. "Just put all the cards directly in front of you, and then you'd have zero cards face up on your left and right side."

"I should've told you that every card must be either on your left or right side."

"Let me think about it. The first step in solving a math problem is to draw a picture, if possible, but in this case using a deck of cards would be best. I'll let you know when I solve it."

———

The next day Gray went to the Department of Motor Vehicles. He walked up to a pale middle-aged woman who worked there and said, "If I give you a license plate number, can you find out who the car is registered to?"

"I could, but I won't," she replied.

Gray sized her up before he replied. She appeared to have a motherly, maybe a grandmotherly look. "Let me tell you why I want this information. Last night I stopped for a red light. A car pulled beside me on my right side and stopped. The driver of the car was pulling a boat. He made a right on red, but didn't allow for the boat being wider than his car. He hit my car, slightly damaging it. He never realized that he hit me and drove off. I jotted down the license plate number."

"Why don't you report this to the police and your insurance company instead of coming here?"

"The driver was a young man, and if I report this to my insurance company, I'm sure his insurance premiums will jump. If I report this to the police, he might be in trouble because he didn't stop. If I could just talk to him, maybe he'd be willing to pay for the damage to my car. Then we wouldn't ever have to go through the insurance company."

"I have a nineteen-year-old son and I know what you mean about having high insurance premiums to pay. It's nice of you to want to help this young man. I'll give you the information you want."

After a few minutes, she said, "The owner of the car is Joseph Masters. He lives at 395 Kitty Avenue, Buffalo, New York."

Gray thanked the lady for the information and went back to Mohlar's apartment.

———

Mohlar had gone to see a man who has been collecting baseball cards since he was a child.

"Dr. Mohlar, it is so good to see you again. Come into my house," Joseph Townsend said.

"Good morning, Mr. Townsend," the detective said as he entered the living room. Mohlar saw to his surprise a house furnished in a most unusual way. Some of the furniture looked cheap and other furniture looked expensive. He noticed a magnificent antique walnut desk, usually the type only purchased by the affluent. The desk sat on an expensive oriental rug that looked like it had been carefully hand woven. The chairs were cheap but modern looking.

"What brings you to my place today?" Townsend asked.

"I'm interested in buying some of your most valuable baseball cards, provided the price is right," Mohlar answered.

"Come into my office. I keep all my baseball cards there."

After they entered his office, Townsend placed a box of baseball cards on his desk. "Which of your cards would you suggest I buy?"

"Dr. Mohlar, I'm going to be very frank with you. I need cash, and I need it soon. I don't want high prices to stop you from buying the cards you want, so I'll sell you any card in my collection for eighty percent of the book value.

"My most valuable card is this Mickey Mantle rookie card," Townsend said while pulling the card out of the box. "The book value of this card is sixty thousand dollars, so this one card will cost you forty-eight thousand dollars."

"I'll buy the Mickey Mantle card," Mohlar replied.

Then a young lady entered the room. "Dad, you have a phone call from Aunt Bonnie," she said, smiling.

Mohlar thought that Miss Townsend was the most beautiful girl he had ever seen. She appeared to be as many years past twenty as he was past thirty. Looking at her, he couldn't help singing in his mind, *Five-foot-two, eyes of blue...*Although her body was perfectly proportioned, his eyes were focused on her face. She had gorgeous long light brown hair, parted down the middle. When she smiled her teeth sparkled like diamonds. She had brilliant blue eyes and a beautiful complexion.

"Dr. Mohlar, this is my daughter, Kay. Excuse me while I take this call. Maybe Kay can entertain you while I'm gone."

"Would you like a drink?" she asked.

"No, thanks."

"Are you a medical doctor?" she asked.

"No. Some people call me Dr. Mohlar because I have a Ph.D. in mathematics." Mohlar noticed that when he said "mathematics," her face lit up and her eyes sparkled.

"Math was my favorite subject when I was in school," she said. "I loved geometry when I took it in tenth grade. I think it's cool that you can prove so many theorems from just a few assumptions and definitions."

Mohlar saw an opportunity to make a good impression on this beautiful girl. "Miss Townsend, if you give me a number, I can tell you almost immediately whether or not the number is divisible by any of the first five prime numbers; in other words, two, three, five, seven, or eleven."

"Please call me Kay, Dr. Mohlar. I can quickly tell if a number is divisible by two or five, but it would take some time for me to determine divisibility by three, seven, or eleven. Let me time you to see how long it takes you to determine if 5,943 is divisible by three."

Immediately, Mohlar said, "It's divisible by three. By the way, you may call me Sam."

Kay picked up a pen from the table and did the calculation. While smiling, she said, "You're right, Sam. How did you so quickly determine that the number is divisible by three? You told me that answer before I had a chance to start my watch."

"This is what you do, Kay. Add up the digits of the number. If the sum of the digits is divisible by three, then the original number is divisible by three; otherwise, the number is not divisible by three. In this case, the sum of the digits is twenty-one, which is divisible by three."

Without saying a word, Kay wrote a proof for the divisibility test for three. She looked up at Mohlar and asked, "Do you see an interesting extension of this proof?"

"With a slight modification of your proof, you can prove a divisibility test for nine."

"That's exactly what I was thinking," Kay responded. "Whenever the sum of the digits is divisible by nine, the original number is divisible by nine. So we can say that 5,943 is not divisible by nine since twenty-one is not divisible by nine."

Mohlar, very much impressed by this, asked, "Did you major in mathematics in college?"

"I didn't go to college," she answered. "When I graduated from high school, I wanted to go, but my family was having financial problems. So for the past three years, I worked full-time at a warehouse for tires and other rubber products to help my family. I also worked part-time at a grocery store. My father wants to sell his baseball card collection so that my sister, Jenny, and I can go to college. Jenny graduated last month from high school and we are going to start together in the fall. I plan to major in math."

Joe Townsend returned and said, "Dr. Mohlar, did you pick out all the cards you'd like to buy?"

"I had a fascinating discussion with your daughter about mathematics, and I forgot to look over your collection of cards. But I'd like to look them over now."

Kay asked, "Sam, would you see me in the living room before you leave? I want to show you a book I've been reading this summer."

After she left the room, Townsend said, "I'm surprised Kay called you by your first name, especially since I introduced you as Dr. Mohlar."

"I told her to call me Sam," Mohlar replied.

"I'd like you to consider buying my 1952 baseball card of Jackie Robinson. Not only was Robinson a great baseball player, but he'll always be remembered as the player who broke the color barrier in baseball."

Mohlar said that he'd buy the Jackie Robinson card and picked out several other valuable rare cards.

"Can you afford to buy these cards? Including the Mickey

Mantle card, the cards you want to buy will cost you more than one hundred thousand dollars."

After Mohlar hit some buttons on his calculator, he wrote a check for one hundred and four thousand dollars and handed it to Joseph Townsend.

"Thank you very much, Dr. Mohlar," Townsend said while placing the check in his wallet.

When Mohlar entered the living room, Joe Townsend stayed in his office and called the bank to make sure there were enough funds in Mohlar's account to cover the check. He was informed that Mohlar's checking account had a balance of one hundred and ten thousand dollars.

Mohlar found that Kay Townsend was taking notes while reading a book. "Is this the book you wanted me to see?" he asked.

"Yes, it is," she replied. "This book is *Elementary Geometry from an Advanced Standpoint,* by Edwin Moise. I've found it to be fascinating. Are you familiar with it?"

"While I was a teaching assistant in graduate school, I used that book for a course I taught. I particularly liked the problems. Do you have any other interests besides mathematics?" Mohlar asked.

"I'm a Christian, and I'm totally committed to do whatever God wants me to do. I believe He wants me to disciple young people. In obedience to God, I've been meeting with six young people for the past two years. We study the Bible once a week for two hours. The group forms the Bible quiz team from my church, and I'm their coach. Once a month we compete with other churches in upstate New York by answering questions from the Bible."

Mohlar replied, "I know very little about Christianity. I became a believer just yesterday morning. Maybe sometime you could explain to me the basic beliefs of the Christian church."

"I'd be glad to do that. And maybe sometime you can tell me the divisibility tests for seven and eleven," she replied.

"Kay, may I have your phone number?" Mohlar asked confidently.

She wrote her phone number on a small card and gave it to

Mohlar. As Mohlar put the card in his wallet, she said, "I bet your wallet is full of girls' telephone numbers."

"Maybe this will help you learn not to place bets. Your phone number is the only number I have in my wallet."

"May I have your phone number?" she asked.

"I'll give you my cell phone number. Kay, would you be interested in having dinner with me tonight? I'd like to take you to a special restaurant I've heard many good reports about."

"I'd like to have dinner with you. What time should I expect you to be here?"

"How about six o'clock?"

"Six would be fine."

As Mohlar left the Townsend house, he knew that he had just talked with the most wonderful girl he had ever met.

TEN

Mohlar arrived back at his apartment, and Gray was already there. When Mohlar told Gray about meeting Kay Townsend, Gray said as he noticed a sparkle in Mohlar's eye, "This is the most excited I ever seen you 'bout meeting a girl."

"Yes, I think she's special. I want to get to know her better. I have a date with her tonight. Would you be willing to take the night shift?"

"Sure, I'd be glad to."

From Mohlar's apartment each took his own car and went to 395 Kitty Avenue. They soon found the car with the license plate number that was still visible on Mohlar's hand. They drove their cars 150 yards down the street so they could see Flood's house.

When Gray entered Mohlar's car, Mohlar showed him the baseball cards he had bought that morning. Mohlar said he wanted to buy cards that would be attractive to Flood when they contacted him.

"These cards must have cost a fortune," Gray said as he looked at a rookie card of Mickey Mantle and a card of Babe Ruth.

"These two cards alone cost seventy-five thousand dollars," Mohlar replied. "Actually, I paid slightly over one hundred thousand dollars for all the cards here. But Clark said not to spare any expense in obtaining good bait. He said that the rare baseball cards never lose their value, and he can get his money back by selling them to a collector he knows."

"What time should I come so you can make your date on time?"

"If you meet me at five, I should have plenty of time. Remember," Mohlar said with an emphatic tone in his voice, "keep me posted on his every move."

"Are you sure?" Gray asked. "You got this hot date. I'd think you wouldn't want to be bothered by every move he makes. I could use my own instincts and just call you if I feel I need to."

"No!" Mohlar spoke with a raised voice. "This man could be dangerous. I want to know everything and decide what's best."

"Okay, you're the boss, but I hope your work doesn't get in the way of this relationship."

———

Mohlar returned to the Townsend house at six o'clock. Joe Townsend told Kay that Mohlar had arrived. She came down the stairs wearing a beautiful red dress, red shoes, and a pearl necklace.

"That dress looks very nice on you," Mohlar said.

"You said earlier today that we will be going to a special restaurant, so I thought I'd wear my best clothes. I only wear this dress for special occasions. Where are we going?"

"I'm not going to tell you now," he whispered with a smile on his face and a twinkle in his eye. "It's a surprise."

As Mohlar and Kay were walking to his car, he asked, "Do you need to be home by a certain time?"

"I should be home early tonight. I have to work tomorrow. But I don't have a curfew, if that's what you wanted to know," Kay answered, as she took a seat in Mohlar's car.

While they were heading toward the expressway, Mohlar's cell phone rang. He continued to drive as he pulled out the phone from his pocket. When Kay saw that he was going to answer the phone while he was driving, she said, "Do you know it's illegal to drive a car while talking on the phone? Pull off the road, and I'll drive while you talk. Keep in mind that I don't know where we are going, so you'll have to tell me the turns to make."

"I often drive while talking on the phone. But if it makes you feel more comfortable, I'll let you drive. Try to move along at a pretty good speed. I made a seven o'clock reservation for dinner. They won't hold it for us if we're late."

I'm such an idiot, Kay thought. *My first date with this guy and I tell him he's breaking the law. Come on, girl, think before you speak.*

Mohlar answered the phone while they switched seats.

"What took you so long to answer the phone?" Gray asked.

"I had to pull off the road before I answered it."

"Flood left his house 'bout five minutes ago. He's heading south on the expressway that runs beside the Niagara River. I'm right behind him."

"Stay with him and keep me informed."

Mohlar hung up the phone and said, "That was my business partner and best friend, Ken Gray. We're private detectives, and we're hired to find someone. After four months of searching for him, we finally found him. I'm going to leave my cell phone on. Ken might need to call me again."

When they were close to their destination, Kay asked, "Where did you meet my father?"

"I met him at a sports card show. I was there hoping to find someone, and your father was there selling baseball cards. Although I didn't want to buy any cards then, I anticipated that I'd want to buy cards in the future, so I asked him for his name and address."

"How long have you been a collector of baseball cards?" Kay asked.

"I've never been a collector. I bought the cards from your father to use as bait."

"What do you mean, 'bait'?"

"The man I'm looking for is an avid collector. If he learns that I have some valuable cards, he may want to buy them. Just as a fish is attracted to bait, this man may be attracted to the baseball cards."

As they were driving along the Niagara River toward Niagara Falls, Kay said, "This is a beautiful drive. I've been to Niagara Falls many times, but I've never taken this route."

"In a few minutes you'll see the rapids and then the falls."

They drove by the falls and went to a high tower on the American side. They rode an elevator to the top of the tower. There they found a restaurant where each table had a spectacular view of the falls.

The detective said to the hostess of the restaurant, "My name is Sam Mohlar. I have a reservation for seven o'clock."

"I see that you have a reservation for two. Please follow me."

As they followed the hostess to a table near a window, Mohlar looked around the room, briefly glancing at everyone in the restaurant. As they walked toward their table, he noticed many men stopped eating, motionless, with food hanging out of their mouths. He knew it was the beautiful lady in the pretty red dress that drew their attention. He took great pride in his dinner date.

The hostess produced two large menus from under her arm. While putting the menus on the table, she said, "Your waitress will be with you soon."

"Sam, I love this view of the falls. Thanks for bringing me here."

"I told you I was going to take you to a special restaurant."

A few minutes later, a chubby, soft-voiced waitress with a pronounced accent appeared and asked, "Would you like cocktails?"

"I'll have a ginger ale," Kay said.

"Make that two," Mohlar added.

"Do you know what you would like to order, or do you need more time to look over the menu?" the waitress asked.

"I want a nice thick steak covered with mushrooms, a baked potato, a chef salad with Italian dressing, and Italian bread. Please bring plenty of butter for the potato and bread," Mohlar said.

As Kay folded the menu, she said, "I'd like the fish fry with French fries and coleslaw. Please bring me some Italian bread too."

After the waitress left, Kay asked, "Do you know the origin of the word 'cocktail'? Its origin is especially interesting to people living in this area."

"Actually, I've only lived in this area for four months, although I've visited here many times. I've lived in Rochester almost all my life. Do you know I've never thought about the origin of the word 'cocktail'?"

"The first time the word was used to mean an alcoholic mixed drink was at the Frontier House Inn in Lewiston. Do you know where that is?"

"It's on the Niagara River," Mohlar answered. "I've eaten there. The restaurant is now a McDonald's."

"I heard that during the Revolutionary War, Betsy Flanagan, a waitress at the inn, worked undercover for the Revolutionaries. She would identify the Loyalists at the inn by placing a rooster's tail feather in each of their drinks. She told them it was a drink she had invented called a 'cocktail.' These cocktails identified to the Revolutionaries who their enemies were, and they would ambush these men after they left the inn. This story was circulated, and now all mixed drinks are called 'cocktails.'"

"That's an interesting story. Some people think my profession is dangerous, but I think Betsy Flanagan's work was more dangerous."

A few minutes later, the waitress returned with their drinks. After Kay sipped her drink, she looked up at Mohlar and asked, "Do you do anything besides private investigation work?"

"I also work for the Rochester Police Department on a per diem basis. Sometimes they call me in on homicide investigations."

"You have an unusual occupation for someone with a Ph.D. in mathematics."

"I'm not the only detective with a Ph.D. A few years ago I met Don Foster, who has a Ph.D. in English. Police detectives, district attorneys, and even FBI agents have asked Foster to help them in investigations."

"I don't know how an expert in English would be able to help these people."

"With Foster it began in 1996, when he was teaching English literature at Vassar College. A controversial book was published called *Primary Colors*. No one knew who wrote the book. Using his expert knowledge of the use of language in writing, Foster concluded that the author of the book was *Newsweek* columnist Joe Klein. Although Klein initially denied writing *Primary Colors*, five months later he admitted that he was the author of the book.

"His most famous investigation occurred in 2001. That year he was asked to help the police, not only with the investigation of the murder of Bob Stevens, but also death threats to many famous people. The same month that anthrax killed Stevens, anthrax was also found in letters sent to U.S. senators and famous news reporters. Each of the letters contained a message. The FBI sent those letters to Foster for his analysis. At that time everyone assumed foreign terrorists sent the poison letters because of the attacks on New York City and Washington, D.C., the previous month. But Foster figured out that an American sent the letters. He told the FBI the name of the man who sent the poison letters.

"I've found my academic training to be useful in my work as well. In mathematics we do detailed analysis of proofs. That training helped me to develop a talent for observing many details in every situation I'm in."

"Can you give me an example of what you're talking about?"

After Mohlar sipped his drink, he said, "I can give you a detailed description of our waitress. She's about five-foot-four inches tall and has blue eyes with a mole under her left eye. She's about thirty years old, has brown curly hair, and is overweight, weighing about two hundred thirty pounds. She's probably married, since she's wearing a wedding ring. Her accent indicates she comes from or near Boston."

"I'll evaluate how good a description this is when our waitress comes back. I want to challenge you. Without turning around, I'd like you to describe the people sitting behind you," Kay said as she looked past Mohlar.

"Since the only time I've seen these people is when we walked to our table, my description of them will not be as detailed as the previous one. There're four people at the table, three females and one male. The two younger females are both teenagers. The two older people are between forty and fifty years old. All four are Japanese. I assume they're tourists, as they speak very little English. In fact, the man is the only one I've heard speak English. He placed the order for all of them."

"I have a feeling you're trying to snow me. I can see that they're of Asian nationality, but how do you know they're Japanese? Maybe they're Korean or Chinese."

"When I was a graduate student, one of my best friends was from Tokyo, Japan. When he returned home for a vacation, I went with him. I learned to speak and understand some Japanese on that trip. I've been listening in on their conversation, and I understand much of what they're saying. To convince you that they're Japanese, I'll ask them in their language where the restrooms are. I expect they'll answer me in Japanese, and I'll follow their directions to the restroom."

Mohlar said a few words to the man, who gave a reply while pointing toward the exit. Mohlar turned, smiled at Kay, and walked to the restroom.

While Mohlar was gone, the waitress delivered their meals. When Mohlar returned, Kay said that she was convinced that he was very observant. She said that the waitress fit his description perfectly. She also was impressed that he could converse with the people sitting behind him in their language.

"Why did you major in math?" Kay asked while placing a napkin on her lap.

"When I was in college, I wasn't a Christian. Actually, I didn't go to any church. However, I had a belief in God. When I studied math, I felt close to God. I liked that feeling, so I took all the math courses I could."

"I don't understand you when you say that you felt close to God."

"Whenever I proved a theorem or read someone else's proof of a theorem, I thought I discovered one of God's secrets. I want to know as many of His secrets as possible, so I keep studying math."

As Kay cut her fish into small pieces, she said, "Now I know what you mean. I remember when my high school geometry teacher proved to my class that the sum of the angles of a triangle is one hundred eighty degrees. I thought that was awesome. Just think about it. Regardless of the type or size of a triangle, the sum of the angles is always the same number."

He chewed the steak in his mouth and swallowed it. Looking admiringly into her eyes, he said, "When you talk, I sense you have a deep love for math."

"I do love math," Kay responded. "When did you know you loved math?"

Mohlar put his fork on his plate, transferred his attention from his food to Kay, and answered, "When I was in sixth grade, I did an experiment that involved four steps. First, I took a string and measured the distance around several circular objects, such as garbage cans, bowls, cups, and coins. I called these numbers 'the arounds.' Second, I used the string to find the longest distance between two points on the circle. I called these numbers 'the acrosses.' Next, I divided 'the arounds' by 'the acrosses' and called these numbers 'the answers.' Finally, I made a table that recorded all those numbers. I was surprised that all numbers in 'the answer' column were approximately the same—a number slightly larger than three. I had to know the answer to this question: If I divide the 'around' by the 'across' of any circle, will I get the same answer? The next day I showed my teacher the table and asked him that question. He told me the answer is 'yes' after he informed me that 'the around' is called 'the circumference' and 'the across' is called 'the diameter' of the circle. He told me 'the answer' is called 'pi.' I was thrilled to have made that discovery. It was then that I started loving math."

"It's amazing that you discovered the value of pi without any help. Did you know that the concept of pi is found in the Bible?" Kay asked.

"I didn't know that."

"The reference is 1 Kings 7:23. I haven't memorized that verse, but it essentially says that a circle had a circumference of thirty cubits and a diameter of ten cubits. Thus the ratio of the circumference to its diameter is three, which is close to the number pi. I like to find references in the Bible that relate to mathematics, especially geometry."

"I hope someday you get a chance to go to college and take some math courses. Maybe if you go to a Christian college, you'll learn of more references in the Bible that relate to mathematics like the one you just told me about."

"After you left my house today, my father said I could start applying to county or state colleges. My first choice would be a Christian college, but he said they're too expensive. When you bought his baseball cards, he said he had enough money to send my sister and me to college. Just like you, I'm going to take as many math courses as I can."

For several minutes they ate in silence. As he buttered his bread, he said, "Yesterday I became a Christian, and I have many questions about the religion. Christians base their beliefs on the Bible. How do you know the Bible is true?"

"I'll answer your question as a mathematician might answer it. What kind of statements do you use when you prove a theorem?"

"I use previously proved theorems, definitions, and axioms," Mohlar answered.

"Do you doubt the truth of the definitions and axioms?" Kay asked.

Mohlar started to put a piece of bread into his mouth, then withdrew it and answered, "No, these statements are assumed to be true." He put the bread in his mouth.

Kay sipped some ginger ale from her glass and then said, "For me, the Bible contains the definitions and axioms I accept. For example, the Bible states that anyone who shows favoritism sins. Since the Bible states that, I believe it to be true." She slowly lowered her glass to the table.

"Do you have any basis for your acceptance of the truth of the Bible other than faith?"

"There're thousands of prophetic statements made in the Bible, and many of them have been fulfilled," Kay answered.

"Are you concerned that some of the prophecies haven't been fulfilled?"

"No, because I faithfully believe that someday all the prophecies will be fulfilled. Many of the prophecies in the Bible relate to Jesus' return to earth. Obviously, these won't be fulfilled until Jesus' return."

"Can you give me a couple of examples of fulfilled prophecies? I'd like to strengthen my belief in the Bible."

"There're so many prophecies in the Bible, it's hard to choose just two." Kay paused and was deep in thought. Mohlar looked into her pretty blue eyes. He saw how intensely she was concentrating so that she could come up with just the right examples. After a few seconds, he started to speak, but decided not to interrupt her thoughts. They were silent for several minutes until she said, "I'll give you examples of two Old Testament prophecies; one fulfilled in the Old Testament, and the other fulfilled in the New Testament."

She took a swallow of ginger ale and continued, "Isaiah, who was an Old Testament prophet, wrote that King Cyrus would rebuild the Jerusalem temple that was destroyed. Ezra wrote about the fulfillment of this prophecy, which occurred about two hundred years after it was given. It's amazing to me that God even told Isaiah that the name of the king would be Cyrus many years before Cyrus was born."

"Maybe it's a case of a self-fulfilling prophecy," Mohlar said as he was chewing a piece of bread. "It could've been that an Israelite king named Cyrus knew of this prophecy and thought it must be referring to him, so he thought that God expected him to rebuild the temple."

"Your theory isn't correct because Cyrus was not an Israelite. In fact, Isaiah wrote in chapter 45 that Cyrus didn't even know God."

Kay paused to put a French fry in her mouth. After she chewed it, she said, "In about 700 BC the prophet Micah predicted that

Jesus would be born in Bethlehem. Micah 5:2 states, 'But you, Bethlehem Ephrathah, though you are small among the clans of Judah, out of you will come for me one who will be ruler over Israel, whose origins are from old, from ancient times.'"

Mohlar had a puzzled look on his face. As he ran his fingers through his hair, he asked, "What did Micah mean when he wrote, 'The ruler over Israel whose origins are from old, from ancient times'?"

"He meant that Jesus existed long before his birth in Bethlehem."

"Do you know if the Bible directly states that Jesus is God?" Mohlar asked.

"The first sentence in the book of John in the Bible says this: 'In the beginning was the Word, and the Word was with God and the Word was God.'"

"That was certainly what I was looking for if we know that 'the Word' means Jesus."

"If you read the first chapter of John, you'll be convinced that 'the Word' refers to Jesus. You should especially note verse 14, 'The Word became flesh and made his dwelling among us.' So if you believe the Bible is true, then you must believe that Jesus is God and that He became a man."

"I wonder why the author referred to Jesus as 'the Word,'" Mohlar said.

"Suppose you were going to make a wheel. You'd try to make it as close to circular as you could. But could you make it perfectly circular?"

"It's impossible to make it perfectly circular," Mohlar answered.

"When you hear the word 'wheel,' you know in your mind what a perfect wheel would look like. Any wheel you see or try to make would fall short of a perfect wheel. Similarly, there is a perfect man, someone without sin, who we can conceptualize. Every person, except Jesus, is an imperfect man because everyone sins. Jesus was a perfect man because He lived a sinless life. I think the Bible referred to Jesus as 'the Word' to show us the life of a perfect man so that we can strive to be like Him. Therefore, Jesus, the perfect man, is 'the Word.' Am I making any sense to you?"

"That makes sense to me," Mohlar said. "I noticed that you've memorized some of the first chapter of John and some from the book of Micah. Have you memorized much from the Bible?"

"When I was in Bible quizzing, I memorized entire books of the Bible. But that was not unusual. In the advanced competitions many of the quizzers had entire books of the Bible memorized."

When they had finished dinner and were waiting for the waitress to give them the check, Mohlar's phone rang.

"Sam, this is Ken. Flood just drove his car into the Hamilton warehouse on the south side of Buffalo. I'd like to know what's going on inside. Should I try to get in?"

"Stay outside the warehouse. He might see you if you go in. Wait for him to leave and follow him."

———

While Gray settled back in his car to wait for Flood to leave the warehouse, Flood put boxes into his car. After loading the trunk of his car, Flood said to a young man with unruly hair standing next to him, "Andrew, I'll be taking my boss to Canada on Wednesday. We should get in to Niagara Falls about two. I'm scheduled to meet with your father about three–thirty."

"This should work out great," Andrew responded. "I'll make the bank delivery with an armed guard about three."

"Why do I have to shoot the guard in the leg?"

"I'd like to see you waste him."

"Why not?" Flood interrupted. "For an extra ten grand I'll blow his brains out."

"That would be a beautiful sight, but Wednesday just shoot him in the leg. Dead men don't talk, and I want him to tell my father everything that happened. Otherwise, he may suspect that I took the loot."

"Why shoot him at all?" Flood asked as he slammed down the trunk door.

"He'll try to follow you if you don't. Besides, my father will understand me taking care of this wounded man instead of trying to follow you."

"Where am I supposed to put the money?"

"When you go into the woods about fifty yards, you'll see a pile of brush on your left. Take out two bundles from the bag; each bundle contains fifty grand. Put the rest under the brush. I'll pick up the bag later. Any other questions?"

"Nope."

Flood got into his car and drove out of the warehouse. Soon Gray's car was behind him.

———

Mohlar and Kay arrived back at Townsend's house at eight–thirty. He thought, *I hate to end this date. How can I extend it?*

"The night is still young. Maybe we could go to a movie," Mohlar suggested.

"I'd like to go to bed early tonight. My boss gave me today off work provided I go in to work two hours early tomorrow."

"Would you like to have dinner with me tomorrow night?" Mohlar asked. "This time you choose the restaurant."

"I'd like that."

It was at this moment that the cell phone in Mohlar's pocket began to beep. *I'd like to smash that phone*, he thought.

"I followed Flood to a racetrack south of Buffalo, but I lost him at the track. I've waited around the betting windows, but I haven't seen him yet. The windows are now open for the fourth race. Don't you think he would've placed a bet by now?"

"Maybe someone is placing his bets. Wait for him there until the windows close for the fourth race. If he hasn't shown up by then, wait for him near his car."

Mohlar turned to Kay and asked, "What time should I pick you up tomorrow?"

"I could be ready by six.

"This morning you said you know the divisibility tests for the first five prime numbers," Kay said. "What's the divisibility test for seven?"

"This test is easy to apply. Double the ones digit and subtract the result from the number formed by the remaining digits. If this difference is divisible by seven, the original number is divisible by seven. If this difference is not divisible by seven, the original number is not divisible by seven."

"Please give me an example."

Mohlar took out a piece of paper and wrote "504" on it. He said, "The ones digit is four. Double four and you get eight. Subtract eight from fifty to obtain forty-two. Since forty-two is divisible by seven, then 504 is also divisible by seven. Do you understand how to apply this test?"

Kay nodded her head, indicating she understood how to apply the divisibility test, and said, "That divisibility test can be used as an aid in reducing fractions."

When Mohlar was about to leave, his cell phone rang.

"Sam, I lost him. His car wasn't where I thought he left it, so I searched the parking lot. There was no trace of Flood's car in the whole parking lot."

"That's okay. We'll try again tomorrow."

Mohlar hung up the phone, looked into Kay's deep blue eyes, and said, "I'll see you tomorrow at six."

ELEVEN

The next day was hot and humid. Mohlar arrived at Kitty Avenue at 7:00 a.m. and parked his car two hundred yards from Flood's house. He assumed Flood was at home because he could see his car parked behind the house. Two hours later Flood opened the living room drapes. Mohlar picked up his binoculars and watched Flood walking through his rooms. At ten the mailman delivered the mail. At noon Flood came out of his house, picked up the mail, and immediately went back into the house. At one he went out the back door and watered his flowers. After he washed his car, he went back into the house, picked up a book, and read it. Mohlar felt drowsy; he closed his eyes and was soon asleep. When he woke up fifteen minutes later, he saw a woman in the house with Flood. Mohlar had never seen her before. She left a half hour later.

When Gray met Mohlar at four to relieve him, Mohlar said, "Flood has been home all day. While I was watching him, I figured out the math puzzle you told me about last Sunday. Do you want me to tell you the solution?"

"I want to figure it out myself."

Twenty minutes after Gray relieved Mohlar, Mohlar was inside his air-conditioned apartment. He showered, shaved, and set his alarm clock for five-thirty. Mohlar got in between the cool sheets of his bed and switched his thinking about Richard Flood to Kay Townsend. Within five minutes he was dreaming about her.

When his alarm sounded, he immediately got out of bed and went to his closet. He selected a dark blue sports coat, gray slacks, and a clean light blue shirt to wear. He tied a new red tie around his shirt collar. Within ten minutes he got in his car, turned on the air conditioner, and headed toward Townsend's house. Traffic was heavy, but Mohlar still arrived before six.

Kay was dressed more casually than the night before. She was wearing dark blue slacks with a short-sleeved red and white blouse.

"Did you decide where we are going to eat?" Mohlar asked.

"The restaurant is about five miles west of here. My sister ate there a few days ago and liked the place. She said the food is excellent and a band plays while you're eating," Kay said, as the cuckoo clock struck six o'clock.

Kay stuffed her wallet and ring of keys into her big leather purse and slung it over her shoulder before they left her house. As they were driving toward the expressway, Mohlar's cell phone rang. Kay said, "If it's okay with you, I'll drive to the restaurant while you talk on the phone."

Mohlar pulled the car off the road, turned on the hazard lights, and switched seats with Kay. As she turned off the hazard lights and pulled back on the highway, the detective said, "Sam Mohlar speaking."

"This is Ken. About an hour ago Flood left his house. I followed him to a mansion on the west side of Buffalo. Then he did something strange. He took some things out of his car and placed them into the trunk of a limousine."

"Was he trying to hide something in the limo?"

"I think so. He just went to the door of the mansion, talked to someone, and returned to the limo. He's now in the driver's seat of the limo waiting for someone."

"Thanks for keeping me informed. Let me know of any new developments."

After Mohlar hung up the phone, he said, "I'm going to leave my phone on. Ken might need to call me again. Our client is going to call me tonight. He told me he'd call me after he takes an inventory of his plant. He always does the inventory by himself, so it may be late when he calls."

Kay responded, "When we do an inventory at our warehouse, my boss insists on two people doing the inventory. He says that ensures accuracy."

"I told him the same sort of thing once, but he said that he likes to do inventories himself so he knows they're accurate."

As they were driving along the Niagara River, Mohlar said, "I think the Niagara River is my favorite river in the world. I've seen and been on many of the great rivers—the Amazon, Nile, Mississippi, and Thames, but none compare to the mighty Niagara. Here the river is calm and pretty. Just a few miles downstream are the mightiest rapids in the whole world."

"I haven't seen as many rivers as you, but I also love the Niagara River."

They found the restaurant and saw elm trees scattered throughout the parking lot. Since all the shady slots were occupied, Kay parked the car in the sun near the entrance to the restaurant. The heat hit them as they stepped from the vehicle because there was an eighteen-degree difference between the temperature inside the air-conditioned car and outside the car.

They entered the restaurant and paused to look over the assortment of pies and cakes on display at the front. Inside the restaurant was a wonderful change from outside. Inside it was cool, almost cold. Outside it was hot and humid. Inside they could hear a band playing. Outside they heard the noise of cars, trucks, and factories.

The band consisted of a drummer, two guitarists, and a keyboardist. The guitarists were singing.

"My sister told me that this band plays all types of music—some old, some new, some soft, some loud. Ever since she told me about this place, I've wanted to come here."

The hostess approached them and asked, "Would you like a table for two?"

"Yes," Mohlar answered. "Could you find us an out-of-the-way table?"

"We have a table for two in a small alcove. You'll feel like you're all by yourself. Follow me, please."

They followed the waitress to a table wrapped in shadows. She put two menus on the table and lit a candle in the middle of the table.

After the waitress left, Kay said, "I've heard this band takes requests from the audience. Do you have a favorite song you'd like them to play?"

"My father and mother's favorite song was 'The Tennessee Waltz.' I'll request that they play it."

After they ordered their dinners, Kay said, "I was very impressed yesterday by how observant you are. Do you think you can teach me to be more observant?"

"I try to picture in my mind everything I see. If I need to recall any details later, I examine this picture in my mind. I don't think I can teach anyone to do that."

"When did you realize you had this unusual talent of observation?"

"When I was in college, I took part in a psychology experiment involving hypnosis. The researcher took me to a room I'd never been in before. He told me to look around the room. After five minutes, he took me to his office. He asked me to tell him everything I saw in the room. I remembered 218 things. Then he hypnotized me and again asked me to tell him everything I saw in the room. I told him exactly the same things under hypnosis as I did before. He told me later that everyone else who participated in the experiment named less than one hundred items. They did better under hypnosis, but still no one named over two hundred items. It was then that I knew I had a talent not many people had."

"Can you think of an exercise I could do to help me be more observant?"

"When I was a kid, my mother used to play a game with me called 'I Spy.' After taking a couple of minutes to look around the room, I'd close my eyes. She'd give me a clue like, 'I spy something blue,' or 'I spy something under the clock.' I'd get up to five guesses to determine what she saw. I'd get a point if I guessed the item. She'd get a point if I didn't guess it. Then we would reverse roles and she'd be the guesser. The first one to get to five points won the game. I think playing that game helped me become more observant."

Soon the waitress came with their dinners. "Would you ask the band to play 'The Tennessee Waltz'?" Mohlar asked.

"Since they're playing the last song before their break, I'll give them your request while they're off," the waitress responded.

"Would you like to dance when they play 'The Tennessee Waltz'?" Mohlar asked.

"I don't know how to dance," Kay answered in a low voice as she looked down at her plate.

"I'm surprised you don't know how to dance. Didn't you go to school dances? Didn't you have dancing in physical education classes?"

Still looking at her plate, she answered, "My father thought it was a sin to dance, so he didn't allow me to go to school dances. When we had dancing in gym classes, I was sent to a study hall because of my father's objections."

"I wouldn't want you to do something you thought was wrong."

She looked into Mohlar's blue eyes and responded, "I said my father thought it was a sin. I actually don't see anything wrong with dancing. I'd dance with you if I knew how."

"I'll teach you to dance. The woman just follows the man's lead. You should put your right hand on my left and put your left hand on my right shoulder. When I want you to go backward, I'll push your right hand back. When I want you to go forward, I'll pull your hand toward me. So as long as you move as I direct, everything will go smoothly."

"I'm willing to give it a try," Kay responded.

The more I see of this girl, the more I like her, Mohlar thought.

"What do you do to get someone to accept Jesus as Savior?" he asked, changing the subject. "I've talked to my friend, Ken, about Jesus, but he's not interested."

"Ask him to go to church with you. The people at church may help your friend to become a Christian."

"He won't go to church with me. He says Christians are hypocrites."

"That's an excuse many people use for not accepting Jesus. They try to hide the real barrier between them and Jesus. For some, it's a bad habit, like smoking; they think they'll have to give it up. Others know they'll have to give up their sinful lifestyle when they come to Jesus. What's the real reason he won't accept Jesus?"

"He desires to live a life of luxury more than anything else. He has always wanted fine clothes, expensive cars, and the best of everything. Maybe he thinks he'll have to give up his desire for these things if he becomes a Christian."

"You might ask him the same question Jesus asked about two thousand years ago: 'What good will it be for a man if he gains the whole world, yet forfeits his soul? Or what can a man give in exchange for his soul?'"

"Where in the Bible is that found?"

"Matthew 16:26."

"When I became a Christian two days ago, I experienced peace within me. I want Ken to accept Christ as his Savior so he can have the same peace I have."

"Can you give me an example of how you're more peaceful now than before you became a Christian?"

"I used to be disturbed by frequent nightmares; one dream has been repeated many times. My nightmares usually involve me desperately trying to get out of a burning room. I'm alone in the room, but yet I hear sounds of many people crying and groaning. With flames all around me, I go to a locked door and I'm unable to open it. I wake up just when I'm about to burn to death. I haven't had a nightmare since I became a Christian, but it's too soon to predict I won't have any more."

"Keep in mind that I have no credentials to support my remarks, but I want to give you my opinion concerning your sleep problem. I think they were emotional in origin, caused by guilt over sins you've committed. You thought you were going to be punished for your sins. When you accepted Jesus as your Savior, you realized He took the punishment for your sins and you will not have to suffer for your sins. I bet you won't have that nightmare anymore. You may have different nightmares, because everyone has nightmares sometimes. I'll pray that God will help you with your sleeping problem."

After they finished eating their dinners, the waitress appeared. "Would you like anything else?" she asked.

"I'd like a ginger ale," Kay said.

"Make that two," the detective added.

"What are some of your interests?" Kay asked.

"I enjoy playing golf, skiing, and doing math and logic puzzles."

"I also like to work on math and logic puzzles. Have you heard any good ones lately?"

"Two days ago I heard a good puzzle that perplexed me for a while, but I solved it three hours before I picked you up this evening," Mohlar answered. "Suppose you're blindfolded and a deck of fifty-two cards is laid out on a table in front of you, with ten cards face up and the rest face down. How would you move the cards so that the same number of cards are face up on your left side as on your right side?"

"Are you allowed to turn cards over?"

"That's allowed."

Kay was deep in thought for a minute before she said, "I've an idea that might work. Move the cards so that there're exactly ten cards in one group on your right side and all the rest are in another group on your left side. If you turn every card over in the group of ten, would that result in having the same number of face-up cards in each group? Let's see if that works. Suppose after you count out ten cards, two cards in that group are face up. That means there're eight face-up cards in the other group. When you turn over all the cards in the small group, eight cards will be face up, the same number of face-up cards in the other group. I think this procedure will work for any situation."

"You solved this puzzle much quicker than I solved it. Your procedure will work for any situation, and I'll explain why. Let X be the number of face-up cards in the small group. Hence, there're 10 - X face-up cards in the large group. When you turn over the cards in the small group, you'll have 10 - X face-up cards in the small group, which matches the number of face-up cards in the large group."

Kay thought, *Why did I solve it so fast? He just got through telling me he took two days to solve it.* "I think I got lucky," she said softly.

The keyboardist announced, "We have a request to play 'The Tennessee Waltz.' I'm sorry we don't know all the words, but we do know the music. The singers will hum the parts they don't know and sing the parts they know. I hope this will be satisfactory to the person who requested the song."

When the band started to play, Mohlar asked, "May I have this dance?"

Kay wiped her lips with her napkin, dropped it on the table, rose, and said, "Sure."

When they reached the middle of the dance floor, they turned and faced each other. Mohlar held her right hand with his left, put his right arm around her slender waist, and smiled. They knew this was a special moment. It was the first time they had ever touched each other. He looked into her deep blue eyes and pulled her hand toward him. She moved forward, but he stood still. They stood motionless on the dance floor.

"All the other couples are moving," Kay said.

"People in Western New York move when they waltz. We're waltzing like people in Central New York."

She rolled her eyes and said, "I think you're giving me a line."

"You're right."

"That's okay. I'm enjoying this."

Mohlar moved even closer to her. He felt her body relax in his arms.

"I'm going to tell the band after the song is over that I liked their rendition of 'The Tennessee Waltz,'" Kay said while putting her head on his shoulder.

"Do you really want to do that? They don't know most of the words."

"They might need some encouragement."

"You're a sweet girl, Kay Townsend."

They stood motionless in each other's arms until the end of the song.

Mohlar accompanied Kay over to the band. He also wanted to say words of encouragement to them. When they returned to their table, they found that their drinks had been delivered.

"What did you have to do to get a Ph.D. in mathematics?"

"I had to do original research. My research was in mathematical statistics. Why do you want to know?"

"Although I'm completely committed to do whatever God wants me to do, I have a dream that someday I, too, will have a Ph.D. in mathematics. Then I want to get a teaching job at a Christian college or university. I want to teach courses in math and the Bible to young Christians. I love those two areas of study, and I think I could help others have a love for them too. But I do know that it's a dream that may never be reached. Maybe I don't have the intelligence to get such an advanced degree. And even if I was able to get the degree, I might not have an opportunity to work at a Christian college. But I'm going to pursue my dream, so I'm interested in knowing what you did to get your degree."

"Kay, you're a dreamer and that is good. You know what you want and you want to find out how to get it. That's an attractive feature about you. I worked on the problem of detecting changes in probability."

"Let's back up a little. How did you choose a topic for research?"

"A professor I took several classes from suggested that I extend some research he had done. His research concentrated on detecting abrupt changes in probability. He gave me some books and articles to read, and I became very interested in the topic. After I fully understood what he did, I extended his work to detecting gradual changes in probability. I outlined a method of determining when a significant change, even a small significant change, occurred. Finally, under his guidance, I wrote a research paper called a dissertation."

"Would you explain your dissertation simply enough so I can understand what you did? Maybe give me an example of how someone might use your method."

"All universities set entrance requirements for their freshman students. Suppose a particular university defines a freshman student to be successful if he obtains a bachelor's degree in five years or less. Based on that definition and the data it obtains concerning their students, that university can determine the chance that an incoming freshman will be successful. Over the years the probability of success may change. The university may have a probability level it wants to maintain. But when does the university change its entrance requirements to obtain that desired probability? My dissertation dealt with a mathematical procedure for determining when the university should change its entrance requirements."

"Your dissertation sounds very interesting."

"The band is playing another waltz. Shall we dance?" Mohlar asked.

Kay finished her ginger ale, put down the glass, and suggested, "Let's dance the Central New York way."

As they walked toward the dance floor, Mohlar took her hand and his fingers entwined hers. When they set up to dance, Mohlar's cell phone rang.

"Hello, this is Elwood Luff. Would you help me investigate a homicide at Clark's plastic plant?"

"Who was killed?"

"A man by the name of Rubenstein."

"Could I pass on this one?"

"I really need you tonight. Dr. Summerville is at a medical convention in Boston this week. I may need someone to estimate the time of death."

"I'll be there in less than two hours."

When Mohlar hung up the phone, he could see sadness in Kay's face. "Kay, I'm sorry, but I have to leave immediately for Rochester. I just received a call from a police detective, and he wants me to help him investigate a homicide."

"Should I call my father to come and get me?"

"No, I'll take you home."

———

When Luff arrived at the plastic company at eight–thirty, he found many people around a body of a man in one of the offices. He was lying in a pool of blood with a bullet hole in his head.

"Did anyone see what happened here?" Luff asked.

No one in the crowd admitted to seeing anything. "Does anyone know this man?" Luff asked.

"His name is David Rubenstein. He works for me," Darren Aderman responded.

"Tell me more about him."

"He works as a chemist in the Research and Development Division of the company, which I head. He was working on a project developing a particularly hard plastic. I had him work late today preparing a patent for the plastic."

"Do you know what time he was shot?"

"No, I don't."

When Mohlar arrived about an hour later, Luff filled him in on what he found out.

"Let's go into Rubenstein's office and examine the crime scene," Mohlar suggested.

The office was twenty by twenty with two six-foot windows. When Mohlar looked out the windows, he could see an office on the second floor of an adjacent building. "Were the windows closed when the body was found?" Mohlar asked.

"The shots couldn't have come from the other building because the windows were closed, and there aren't any bullet holes in the windows," Luff answered.

Many diplomas and awards were framed and hung on the walls. Obviously, Rubenstein was a highly educated man who had accomplished much in his field.

"Is the body still warm?" Mohlar asked.

"Yes. Please give us an estimate of the time of death," Luff requested. "Since no one saw the shooting, this information will be very important to our investigation."

After taking a few moments to look at the body, Mohlar said, "I can give you an estimate for the time of death, but you should realize that his death was probably not instantaneous. I would guess he became unconscious immediately following being shot because there was no sign of him trying to phone for help."

"Why do you think his death was not instantaneous?" Luff asked.

"The victim was lying in an unusually large pool of blood. This is evidence that despite the victim's unconsciousness, his heart continued to pump blood throughout his body. He may have died ten minutes after being shot or he may have died forty-five minutes after being shot. I don't know."

"Well, at any rate would you give me an estimate of the time of death?" Luff asked.

"Of course," Mohlar replied.

"How do you figure that out?" Aderman asked.

As Mohlar was collecting data, he answered, "There're only three pieces of data needed to determine when someone dies. The first is the temperature of the body. The second is the exact time the temperature was taken. The third is the temperature of the room the corpse is in. Using Newton's Law of Cooling and elementary calculus, the time of death can be determined."

"But when I watch court cases on television, an interval is given for the time of death."

"I also give an interval for the time of death," Mohlar replied.

"In statistics that is called a confidence interval. A confidence interval is needed because not everyone's normal body temperature is the same, and the measuring devices may not be accurate. I usually give the police a ninety-five percent confidence interval."

"So you are saying there will be a five percent chance of error in the interval you give the police."

"That's correct," Mohlar responded.

Aderman rubbed his hand on his chin and with a quizzical look on his face asked, "What happens to your time interval if you cut down your chance of error?"

"The smaller the chance of error, the larger the interval for the time of death," Mohlar answered.

After taking several measurements and doing some calculations, he reported that he was ninety-five percent confident that Rubenstein died at 7:40—give or take twenty minutes.

As Mohlar looked over the crowd, he saw a man standing a full head above the rest. He immediately walked over to him and asked, "Raymond, what do you know about David Rubenstein, and what does he do here?"

"My mother-in-law hired him as the head chemist for the company almost three years ago. My brother-in-law, Darren Aderman, was upset without cause that she hired him. You see, Rubenstein is a Jew, and Darren hates Jews. Aderman was his boss, and there has been constant conflict between the two of them ever since Rubenstein joined the company. But Rubenstein was a brilliant chemist and she wouldn't fire him. I'm glad she didn't. He and his assistant, William Howe, just developed the world's strongest plastic that we'll soon put into production."

"I was told that Rubenstein was shot while working in his office. Did you hear a gunshot tonight?" Mohlar asked.

"As you know, I was doing an inventory of the plant tonight," Clark responded. "I think I would've heard a gunshot, unless a silencer was used.

"I'm sorry to change the subject, but would you give me a progress report on Flood?"

"Gray has been following him tonight. He found out that he's working as a chauffeur for a man in Buffalo. I expect we'll contact him soon. Of course, I'll give you daily reports on our progress. Do you know why someone would kill Rubenstein?" Mohlar inquired.

Clark ran his tongue across his lips, swallowed, and answered, "Some people hate Jews. That's possibly why he was killed."

"Do you know where I can find Howe?"

"He's the man next to the water cooler lighting up a cigarette."

Mohlar walked over to Howe and said, "My name is Sam Mohlar, and I'm working with the Rochester Police Department in the investigation of the murder of David Rubenstein. Do you know anyone who hated Rubenstein?"

"Everyone around here knows that our boss, Darren Aderman, didn't get along with David. I don't know if it was that Mr. Aderman hated Dave or if their personalities clashed or both, but there was almost constant conflict between the two of them. Mr. Aderman often yelled at him about always wanting more money to do our research. I can't think of anyone else who disliked Dave."

"Were you working with Dr. Rubenstein tonight?"

"We've developed a new plastic. Mr. Aderman wanted us to write up a patent proposal as soon as possible to protect the company's rights to it. Dave wanted to delay writing the proposal until we did further research. That caused a fight yesterday between Mr. Aderman and Dave. Mr. Aderman's wishes prevailed, so we were writing the proposal this evening."

"What research was there left to do?" Mohlar asked.

"Why do you want to know?"

"Maybe the motive for this homicide was not hatred. Maybe the motive had something to do with this research project. I can understand your reluctance to answer my question. I give you my word that the only people I'll repeat this to are the police detectives."

"Our company buys petroleum from two companies, the Dunsford Petroleum Company and the Lewis Petroleum Company. In all of our tests, we used the petroleum from Dunsford. Dr.

Rubenstein wanted to find out if we would get a harder plastic if we used Lewis's petroleum. But I guess the company ran out of Lewis's petroleum because each time we requested the petroleum, we were told none was available. There may have been other research Dr. Rubenstein wanted to do that I wasn't aware of. Mr. Aderman didn't want to wait any longer to write the proposal. Dave told me that we would finish the research on the plastic after we wrote the patent proposal."

"When was the last time you saw Dr. Rubenstein today?"

"I left Dave about six this evening. We hadn't finished writing the proposal when I left. Dave said that he'd complete the proposal before he went home. About eight-thirty tonight Mr. Aderman called me and told me that someone had shot and killed Dr. Rubenstein."

"Can you think of anything else that might help us with this investigation?"

"No."

Mohlar dialed Gray's cell phone number. "Hello, Ken. This is Sam. I'm in Rochester now, so it'll be late when I get home. I'll take the first shift tomorrow."

"Okay, I'll see you tomorrow," Gray said.

Mohlar hung up the phone and went to his apartment. While he was considering taking a cold shower, he sank into a deep sleep.

TWELVE

Mohlar drove by Flood's house a few minutes after seven the next morning and noticed his car parked on the street. Mohlar parked his car where he could easily see Flood's house and car.

After leaving Townsend's house Monday afternoon, he bought a Bible. He took it out of the glove compartment of his car and started reading the book of Matthew. He knew he had to read something interesting or he'd fall asleep.

Three hours later Gray arrived. He walked over to Mohlar's car and got in. Although they had followed many people by car, they reviewed the procedure so they would not lose Flood on the highway.

"Keep in mind there are two of us following him," Mohlar said. "If we suspect that he knows we are following him, the one closest to him should drop out. Don't always keep a fixed distance behind him. When he slows up, you can stay farther behind him than normal."

"Don't sweat it, Sam. I know how to shadow people."

"Ken, it has taken us four months to find this elusive chauffeur. I don't want to have to go back to square one."

Two hours later Flood, in a navy blue uniform and carrying two suitcases, left his house. Immediately upon seeing Flood, Gray left Mohlar's car and entered his own. Flood quickly got into his car and took off with screeching tires toward downtown Buffalo. A few seconds later, Mohlar and Gray were behind him.

Soon Gray called Mohlar and said, "It looks like Flood is heading toward the mansion I followed him to last night. Since I know right where it is, why don't ya drop out for now. I'll call you when he leaves the mansion."

Mohlar was pleased to drop out because he was hungry and welcomed a chance to eat lunch. He entered a small diner and ordered bacon, eggs, hash browns, and orange juice. While he was waiting for his order to be served, he watched his waitress make sandwiches. She made three tuna salad, three chicken salad, and four roast beef sandwiches.

After she wrapped and put the last sandwich in the refrigerator, she delivered Mohlar's order. Even though the food was excessively greasy, he hurriedly ate everything on his plate.

Just after he finished eating, Mohlar's cell phone rang. Thinking Gray was calling back, he said, "Hello, Ken. This is Sam."

"Sam, this is Elwood Luff. I just wanted you to know about an important development in the Rubenstein homicide investigation. A security officer saw Hattie Aderman, Darren Aderman's wife, cleaning up Rubenstein's office about the time you figured Rubenstein died. I'm guessing she was wiping off fingerprints."

"That explains why we couldn't find any fingerprints last night," Mohlar added. "Thanks for keeping me informed."

———

Gray followed Flood to the same place he had followed him yesterday. Flood put his two suitcases into the trunk of a limousine and then went to the front door of the mansion. He briefly talked to someone and then returned to the limousine. About fifteen minutes later, a well-dressed couple came out of the mansion. Flood got out of the limousine and opened its back door. The couple entered the back and sank into the heavy leather seats. Flood hurried around the back of the limousine and got behind the wheel. He drove the big shining car toward the expressway. A few seconds later, Gray's car, with barely an audible hum of the engine, moved in the same direction. After Gray caught up to them on the expressway, he called Mohlar and said, "Sam, I'm behind Flood, and he's heading toward the Grand Island Bridge. I'm having no difficulty following him."

"I'll soon be behind you," Mohlar said.

Mohlar and Gray followed Flood for about twenty miles to Niagara Falls. Flood drove to the end of one of three long lines going into Canada. Mohlar and Gray went into each of the other two lines.

After a few minutes, Gray called Mohlar and said, "I'm afraid we're going to lose him—my line is moving much slower than his."

"You might be right, but it just takes one of us to get through before Flood."

Then Mohlar's line started moving faster than the other two lines. The car ahead of Flood's car was delayed for inspection. The Customs Inspector opened the trunk of the car. He carefully examined every item in the trunk. This delay allowed Mohlar to arrive at Customs before Flood.

"Citizenship?" the Customs Inspector asked Mohlar.

"U.S.A."

"Where are you going in Canada?"

"Niagara Falls, Ontario," Mohlar answered.

"For what purpose are you entering Canada?"

To catch a murderer, thought Mohlar. "Sightseeing," Mohlar told him.

"How long do you plan on being in Canada?"

"A day or two."

As Mohlar drove off, he looked back to see where Flood and Gray were. Flood was driving up to the Customs Inspector, and Gray was still waiting in line. Mohlar pulled his car off to the side of the road and waited for Flood to pass through Customs.

Mohlar followed Flood through the streets of Niagara Falls, Ontario, while Gray was delayed at Customs. It was a beautiful city with a government that strove to appeal to tourists. Gardens with many pretty flowers made the area near the falls beautiful. Public buildings were recently painted, and clutter was not allowed to remain on the streets. This time of year the city attracted many tourists.

Mohlar noticed Canada's close ties with Great Britain; many of the public buildings were decked with the flags of both countries. Flood stopped at the Movieland Wax Museum to let out his passengers. He then drove to a nearby motel.

Mohlar called Gray and said, "Flood is checking into a motel. There's a motel across the street, but if we contact him today, we may not need to stay. What do you think?"

"We might not be able to make contact with him today. If we don't check in now, we might not be able to get rooms in that motel later. It's important to get rooms close to his. Money seems to be no object in this case."

"Are you still having trouble getting through Customs?"

"Yeah, my line is moving so slow. They're checking every car."

While Flood was checking into the motel, Mohlar checked into the motel across the road. He paid for two rooms—his room and Gray's room. The rooms were small and smelled of smoke. The carpets were badly worn. Nevertheless, he liked the location of the rooms because Flood's room was visible from each room.

Mohlar pulled up a chair to the window of his room. He could see the rapids of the Niagara River as he sat in his chair. He could also see Flood's room. While he was sitting in his comfortable chair, he became sleepy. In five minutes he was sound asleep.

Mohlar woke to knocking at the door. When he looked at his watch, he was surprised that it was three-fifteen. He had slept for an hour. No harm done, he thought, since Flood's car is in the same place it was an hour ago.

Mohlar opened the door and saw the motel manager standing there. "Mr. Mohlar, I failed to tell you that we have a weekly rate that will amount to a big savings over renting day by day. Would you and your friend be interested in our weekly rate?"

"We prefer renting by the day. We don't know how long we'll stay in Niagara Falls."

"If there's anything you need, please let me know."

Three minutes after Mohlar woke up, Flood left his room and started walking downtown.

Mohlar called Gray and said, "I registered you in room seven of the Partridge Motel on Treadwell Street. Flood rented room twelve of the motel across the road. Find out the name that Flood used when he rented the room. We may be here a few days, so pick up some things we'll need. I'm going to follow Flood. He's walking downtown."

"Sam, I'm on Third Street and I got a problem. My car died and I'm gonna let it sit for a while. I'll need some cash before I go to the store."

"You're close to the motel," Mohlar said. "Walk two blocks west and you'll be at Treadwell. After you make a left and walk four or five blocks, you'll see the Partridge Motel on your right. Do you think you can pick the lock of my car?"

"No problem," Gray answered.

"Good. After I put your motel key, my car keys, and a hundred dollars in the glove compartment of my car, I'll lock the car doors. You can use my car to get the needed supplies. We'll get your car later. I need to concentrate on catching up with Flood, so I'll talk to you later."

Mohlar followed Flood to the local casino. When Mohlar walked into the casino, he saw Flood walking toward the back. Flood opened a door having the word *Private* printed on it. He closed the door while entering the room.

Mohlar walked out of the casino and called Gray. "I followed Flood to the casino. I'll try to talk to him and see if I can set up a time and place to show him the baseball cards."

"Good luck," Gray replied. "This is a dump of a motel we're staying in."

"I picked the motel because of its location, not because of luxury."

When Mohlar walked back into the casino, he saw Flood standing by the roulette wheel, taking notes. Twenty minutes later Flood started to play roulette. He always bet that the ball would fall into a 19–36 slot; he always bet high. Usually, he lost his bet. After a while, he walked over to the bar and ordered a drink. He pulled out a calculator from his shirt pocket and hit some buttons.

Mohlar walked to the bar and said to Flood, "How are things going?"

"Not good. I've been playing roulette for some time this afternoon. Every time I bet the high numbers, and I've won only thirty percent of the time. But the rules of probability say I should've won about forty-seven percent of the time. The Law of Averages states that soon the high numbers will win more often to catch up to the low numbers."

Mohlar replied, "I'm a mathematician, and I can tell you it doesn't work that way. The Law of Averages states that when an experiment, such as spinning a roulette wheel, is done many times, the probability of success tends to be close to the actual probability. But the roulette wheel has no memory and so it doesn't feel like it has to catch up. So what I'm saying is that the probability of a high number winning on the next spin is the same for every spin. A statistician can't predict what will happen on the next spin of the roulette wheel, but he can predict approximately what percent of the spins of the roulette wheel the ball will land in slots 19–36, provided the wheel is spun a large number of times."

Flood showed he didn't understand this mathematical principle when he said, "The ball has just landed on a low number slot for the fourth consecutive time. I figure the ball will land in slots 19–36 with much more regularity now. Got to go back to the roulette wheel and start betting the high numbers."

When Flood returned to the roulette wheel, Mohlar went to the restroom. He suddenly felt sick. He wished he had not eaten all that greasy food for lunch. After a few minutes, Mohlar called Gray and said, "I talked to Flood, but I didn't get a chance to set the trap. I feel sick now, so I want you to come to the casino and set the trap. I'm going to walk back to the motel room and rest for a while."

"I'll be at the casino in a few minutes," Gray said. "I found out that Flood is staying at the motel using the name of Joseph Masters. Is that the name he gave you at the casino?"

"He didn't give me his name," Mohlar answered.

As Mohlar walked along, he felt very sick. He saw a wooded area about a half block away. He walked behind some bushes so he'd be out of sight if he had to vomit. When he felt better, he started to walk out of the wooded area. He saw a large bag behind a bush. He walked over, picked it up, and looked inside. He was surprised to see the bag was full of money, all of it in cash. When he looked over the cash, he estimated that the bag contained many hundreds of thousands of dollars.

Mohlar immediately called Gray and said, "Ken, I found something that will change our lives. Leave the casino immediately and meet me back at the motel."

"Flood just went back to the bar for a drink. I might have a chance to talk to him now," Gray replied.

"Ken, I want to see you right away. We can lay the bait for Flood some other time."

THIRTEEN

Gray reached the motel soon after Mohlar arrived. With excitement in his eyes and voice, he asked, "What's up? Why did ya want to see me?"

Mohlar answered as he was showing Gray the bag, "Look what I found not too far from here."

Mohlar dumped all the money out on the bed and they started counting it. All the time they were counting the money, Gray was singing "We're in the Money." Finally Mohlar said, "So this totals six hundred thousand dollars, half of it for each of us."

"It's nice that you want to split the money, but you're the one who found it. It all belongs to you."

"No, we can split the money. I found it because you relieved me at the casino."

Smiling, Gray said, "Won't never have to work again. We can put the money in the bank and live off the interest. We can retire after we finish the job we're working on now."

Suddenly, Mohlar put his hands on his cheeks and thought, *What have I been thinking? This isn't right. It's not my money. Only three days ago I committed my life to Jesus and here I am acting like my old self. Didn't Jesus make me a new creature? I have to try to find the owner of this money and give it back.*

Gray was so excited about finding the money that he didn't notice Mohlar's distress. He was dancing and singing and praising Mohlar, while his friend was deep in thought.

Finally, Mohlar said, "Ken, I think we should give the money to the police so they can find out who it belongs to."

Gray continued twirling and swaying, but stopped singing and praising. He never heard a word that Mohlar said.

"Ken! Ken!" Mohlar shouted.

"What?"

"I think we should give the money to the police so they can find out whom it belongs to."

Gray was no longer smiling. "Are you crazy?" he asked, stunned. "That's an un-American thing to do."

"Why?" Mohlar asked.

"'Cause we can take the Canadian funds and invest the money in our country. That will help our economy."

"But the money isn't ours. We need to do what's right and return it."

"So you return your half and I'll keep mine."

"If I do that, whoever tries to claim the money will say I'm holding out on him. I wish I never found the money. But since I found the money, I should have the deciding vote on what to do with it. I vote to return it," Mohlar stated as he stared out the window.

"I can't go with you. The sight of losing all my money will be too painful."

Mohlar's eyes became wide as he said, "Look! Flood just came back. I wonder where he got that Pontiac he's driving."

After a few minutes, Gray said, "He's taking boxes out of the limousine and is putting them into the Pontiac. They look like the boxes he put into the limousine yesterday."

"Can you see the license number of the Pontiac?" Mohlar asked.

Gray put binoculars over his eyes and said, "It's an Ontario license plate, number 7156RH."

For fifteen minutes the two detectives watched every move Flood made. When Flood got into the Pontiac, Mohlar said, "While he's gone and after it's dark, I want you to get into his motel room and take a picture of anything I might be interested in seeing. I'll follow Flood and try to find out what is in the Pontiac and who owns the car."

———

The next morning Mohlar woke to a knocking at the door. He quickly dressed and opened the door.

"Good morning, Sam," Gray said. "I took these pictures, but I didn't find anything of interest in Flood's room."

Mohlar looked over the pictures and agreed with Gray. Mohlar said, "Last night Flood drove into a white warehouse on the south side of the city. By the time I could sneak into the warehouse, the boxes were unloaded, and I don't know where they were put."

Later that morning Mohlar went to the Niagara Falls Ontario Police Department to return the money. Mohlar approached a young officer and said, "My name is Samuel Mohlar. Yesterday I found this bag full of money. I want to return it to the owner. Would you find out whose money this is?"

"Actually, someone came to the police station about an hour ago and said that he lost a great deal of money. How much money is in the bag?"

"Six hundred thousand dollars," Mohlar replied.

"Are you sure you counted the money correctly?"

"I counted the money twice. Each time I counted six hundred thousand dollars."

"Stay here for a while because we'll want to count the money to make sure," the young officer said.

Mohlar sat in a well-padded chair and watched the policemen work. He saw the young officer make a telephone call while two other officers counted the money. He watched a fourth officer, who was considerably older than the other three, take care of a steady flow of people seeking help. One man was mugged and his wallet was stolen. Another man's car was broken into and his camera was taken. Both were told that the police could do little to help. The rest of the complaints involved violations of traffic and parking laws.

After watching this impatient, unsympathetic, patronizing officer work for forty-five minutes, Mohlar was pleased to see the young officer walking toward him. On the officer's left was a short, heavy man with wide shoulders and a thick neck. Mohlar was surprised to see no gray hair on a man in his early fifties. His head was nicely tanned and cleanly shaved with a styled haircut. His navy blue suit was new, expensive, and tailor-made. The officer said, "Samuel Mohlar, this is Randy Hamilton. We believe that he lost the money you found. We have a problem here. Mr. Hamilton, how much money did you put in the moneybag?" the officer asked.

"Seven hundred thousand dollars," Hamilton answered, stressing each word.

"Are you sure?" the officer asked.

"I'm positive. My wife and I each counted the money."

"Who did you give the moneybag to?" the officer asked.

"My son, Andrew. I asked him to deposit the money in the bank. I sent my assistant, Henry Scott, as a bodyguard for Andrew."

"What happened to the moneybag?" the officer asked.

"They took an armored car and parked it two blocks from the bank. While they were walking toward the bank, a man carrying a gun attacked them. He shot Scott in the leg, grabbed the moneybag, and ran into a wooded area. Andrew helped Scott to the hospital rather than going after the robber."

"I think the gunshot would've aroused the attention of other people," the officer said. "Did those people see the robber?"

"The robber had a silencer on the gun, so the shot didn't arouse attention. The only people who saw the robber were my son and my assistant."

"See if he can identify the bag," Mohlar said.

The officer replied as his eyes shifted from Hamilton to Mohlar, "He has—right down to the bald eagle with its wings spread out and the snow-capped mountains in the background."

Turning back to Hamilton, the officer said, "You told me before someone robbed your assistant and your son while taking your money to the bank. They described the thief to be about five-foot-eight and about one hundred eighty pounds. Did they say anything about his face?"

"They said his face was covered with a mask, but they could see his eyes were blue."

The officer's eyes moved to focus on Mohlar. Only his eyes moved. After staring at Mohlar for ten seconds, he said, "Mr. Mohlar, will you step on the scales?" After noting his weight, the officer measured his height.

"Mr. Mohlar, you're five-foot-nine, weigh one hundred seventy-seven pounds, and have blue eyes. I'd say you fit the description of the robber."

"So do thousands of other people. I'm not the robber. If I were the robber, why would I return the money?"

As the officer turned toward Hamilton, Randy's eyes appeared hot under a reddening forehead. The officer said, "I don't understand what happened to the missing money. Mr. Hamilton, before you leave, please give me the address and phone number of both your assistant and your son. I have some questions for them."

Hamilton's nostrils moved in and out with his breathing. "I know what happened to it," Hamilton said with his eyes staring belligerently into Mohlar's face. "That crook Mohlar took it. He stole one hundred grand from me." Then Hamilton took a swing at Mohlar, but Mohlar stepped back, avoiding being hit. Immediately the officer grabbed Hamilton and threw him to the floor. The officer twisted Hamilton's right arm across his back so hard that Hamilton thought it was going to break.

The police officer said, "If he took the money, why did he come here today? He could've taken all of it and he never would've been caught."

Speaking in pain, Hamilton said, "Sorry I accused you of stealing money from me. I should be grateful to you for recovering almost all the money I lost."

"That's all right," Mohlar said. "I'm sorry you lost some money, but I want to assure you that I returned all the money I found."

"I believe you, Mohlar. I want to reward you for finding my money," Hamilton said making an effort to smile. "I'm the primary owner of a casino in town. I'd like to give you a day of enjoyment at my casino. Tomorrow I'll pay for all the food you want to eat and give you a C-note to play the games."

"Thank you, but you don't have to do that," Mohlar replied. "Besides, I don't like to gamble."

"But I want to do this for you. And it isn't gambling when you play with my money."

"All right, I'll be there tomorrow."

FOURTEEN

When Mohlar saw Gray that afternoon, he told Gray what happened at the police station.

"I have a bad feeling about this man Hamilton. People usually don't blow up one minute and be thankful the next. I think I'll keep an eye on you at the casino. If you think you might be in danger, give me the usual signal and I'll get you out of trouble," Gray said.

"I don't think he could do anything to me in the casino, but I'd feel better having you watch me."

Gray woke up to his alarm clock the next morning. He threw off his pajamas and took a long hot bath. After he got out of the bathtub, he went back to bed. He remained there for an hour thinking about what he could have done with the three hundred thousand dollars if Mohlar had agreed to split the money with him. He rose from bed at fifteen minutes before nine and dressed, wishing he could see the colors of the clothes he put on. As he tied his thin black tie, he thought for a moment about his sports coat. *Is it a loose enough fit to conceal my revolver?*

He opened his dresser drawer and took out a leather holster. He slipped it over his left shoulder, and it hung about two inches below his armpit. He reached into the drawer again and pulled out a .22 Winchester automatic revolver with a thin grip. He loaded the weapon, put on the safety catch, and placed it into the shallow pouch of the shoulder holster. He slipped on his light blue sports coat over his white silk dress shirt. He looked in the mirror to see if there was any sign of the flat gun under his left arm. He was pleased that there was no sign. He walked out of his motel room and locked the door.

As planned, Gray arrived at the casino before Mohlar. Gray ordered bacon, fried eggs, toast, and coffee. He soon consumed it all. He ordered a large glass of orange juice. He drank it down, leaving the corners of his mouth orange.

A few minutes later, Mohlar arrived at the casino. He immediately went to the restroom. Gray followed him in. Since they weren't alone, Gray gave him a signal to let him know he was armed. Mohlar acknowledged his signal and gave a return signal that Gray needed to wash the orange juice off his face. He was glad that Mohlar noticed the orange juice because he wanted to be as inconspicuous as possible.

Soon after Mohlar left the restroom, he saw three people walking toward him. To his left was Hamilton, in the middle was an attractive middle-aged woman, and to his right was a young undersized man with unruly hair. The woman had short black hair that was parted down the middle. Her well-developed tan made her blue eyes vivid and her teeth very white.

"Good morning, Mr. Mohlar," Randy Hamilton said. "This is my wife, Rosie, and my son, Andrew. We want you to have a very nice day at our casino. Andrew will be your personal waiter for the day. Anytime you want something to eat or drink, you let him know and he'll get it for you. And here is one hundred dollars to use at the games. Do you have any questions?"

"No questions. Thank you very much for giving me this special day."

Throughout the day, Gray stood some distance away. In the early afternoon Mohlar went to the restroom, and Gray followed him in. Mohlar informed Gray that his personal waiter was Andrew Hamilton, Randy Hamilton's son. Mohlar and Gray left the restroom separately so that no one would suspect that they were together.

In the evening, Mohlar saw a tall, swarthy stranger limping toward him. His arms and chest bulged with muscles, and he had absolutely no hair on his head. He stopped, motioned to Mohlar, and said, "Yo, come here."

Mohlar walked over to him and asked, "What's up?"

"My name is Henry Scott, and I'm Mr. Hamilton's assistant. Mr. and Mrs. Hamilton wish to see you in their office."

Then Mohlar touched his beard with his left hand and looked toward Gray to see if he had caught his signal. Gray touched his beard with his left hand to let Mohlar know he had.

Mohlar said, "Let me finish my ginger ale, and then I'll go with you." He deliberately drank his ginger ale slowly.

After Mohlar finished his drink, he followed Scott down the dimly lit hallway until they stood at a frosted glass door. Mohlar recognized the room as the same room Flood entered yesterday. "After you," Scott said as he opened the door.

Randy and Rosie Hamilton were waiting inside for Mohlar. When Mohlar entered the room, Scott grabbed Mohlar from behind. Scott put his right hand over Mohlar's mouth while stretching his left arm around Mohlar's arms so that they were unable to move. Randy Hamilton quickly pulled a needle out of his pocket and stuck it in Mohlar's right arm. Mohlar kicked his right foot backward, striking Scott's right leg. Scott grimaced in pain and loosened his grip on Mohlar's mouth and arms. Mohlar twisted his body to the left, raised his left elbow, and struck Scott under the chin. Then Mohlar threw a hard right hook, which landed on Scott's left jaw. As Scott fell to the floor, Randy Hamilton grabbed Mohlar from behind.

Suddenly, Mohlar felt weak from the drug injected in his arm. In an attempt to see better, he quickly closed and opened his eyes three times. Although everything was blurry, he could still see the door. He tried to move toward it, but Hamilton pulled him back. As Mohlar attempted to kick his right leg backwards, he found it wouldn't move. After straining to kick Hamilton with his left leg, Mohlar discovered it wouldn't move either. Soon Mohlar fell asleep in Hamilton's arms.

The Hamiltons and Scott carried Mohlar to a car located in the rear of the casino and put him in the trunk. They drove slowly for two miles down a winding road that led to a large white warehouse on the south side of the city.

To the east of the white building, the rapids of the Niagara River were visible. The roar of the falls was constant and loud, but Mohlar heard nothing.

Scott pulled Mohlar, still unconscious, out of the trunk of the car. Scott and the Hamiltons carried Mohlar into the building and put him in a chair. Rosie Hamilton took Mohlar's wrist between her index finger and thumb and felt for his pulse. Then she dropped his wrist and settled back in a chair while her husband lit a cigarette. They waited for Mohlar to regain consciousness.

After a few minutes, Mohlar opened his eyes and saw a blurred image of someone holding something. After Mohlar blinked a few times to sharpen his vision, he realized that Henry Scott was pointing a revolver at him.

"How long have I been unconscious?"

"About fifteen minutes," Rosie Hamilton answered.

"Don't answer his questions," Randy said, his cigarette in the corner of his mouth. "Mohlar, I want the hundred grand you snatched from the moneybag."

"I told you that I returned to you all the money I found."

Hamilton glowered at Mohlar, hit him with an open hand, and said, "Give me your wallet."

Mohlar fell to his knees. Rosie reached into his hip pocket, pulled out his soft leather wallet, and handed it over to her husband. "You're not going to find one hundred thousand dollars in the wallet if that's what you think," Mohlar said as he struggled to his feet.

While Hamilton handed his wife the wallet, he said, "Rosie, maybe you'd like to go into the other room. Some blood might flow in here. See if there's anything in Mohlar's wallet that will tell us where the loot is. Photocopy everything you find in it."

Hamilton turned to Scott and said, "Tie his hands together, tie him to the chair, and then beat the information out of him."

"Don't you think I would've told you where the money was if I had it when Scott pointed a gun at my head? I don't understand why you don't believe me."

Hamilton replied, "I don't believe you because I put seven hundred grand in the bag and you returned it to me with six hundred grand. Clearly, you kept a hundred grand."

"Maybe whoever was taking care of the money for you took it," Mohlar replied.

"Impossible," Hamilton answered. "I completely trust the men who were taking the money to the bank."

As Scott tied up Mohlar, Hamilton lit a cigarette. While Scott went to get his club, Hamilton repeatedly tapped the ashes of the cigarette into an ashtray. When Scott returned with a club in his hand, Hamilton pinched out the cigarette and lit up another one. Mohlar, resting with his eyes closed, was unaware that Scott had returned. As Scott raised the club to strike Mohlar, Hamilton started ed nervously tapping the cigarette on the edge of the ashtray. Scott viciously struck Mohlar in the back of the head with the club, and Mohlar blacked out. Hamilton dropped the cigarette in the ashtray as he watched Scott raise the club again. When Scott hit Mohlar in the back, he raised his head and regained consciousness.

Scott dropped the club, put a padded glove on his hand, and hit Mohlar in the mouth. As blood was flowing from his lip, the detective said, "Wait, I've something to tell you."

Immediately Hamilton said, "Stop hitting him. Mohlar, where's the money?"

"It appears that Scott will beat me until I die since I don't know where the money is. Hamilton, isn't your soul worth more than one hundred thousand dollars? Jesus asked, 'What good will it be for a man if he gains the whole world, yet forfeits his soul?'"

"I might ask you the same question," Hamilton said. "Stealing is also a sin. But it isn't just the hundred grand. Mr. Mohlar, many people work for me. If I let you get away with stealing my money, how many of my employees will try to steal from me?" Then

Hamilton said with an air of cockiness, "I want everyone to know it doesn't pay to steal from Randy Hamilton."

Mohlar could see that Hamilton desired to dominate everyone around him. Hamilton wanted them to yield to his power.

"Scott, beat him."

As Scott pulled back the club to hit Mohlar, the detective said, "Wait, I've something else to tell you. When I went to your office at the casino, my friend kidnapped your son, Andrew. If you kill me, he'll kill Andrew."

"I don't believe you. If that really did happen, why didn't you tell me as soon as possible?"

"I wanted to give my friend enough time to abduct your son."

"Too many people around the casino for that to happen," Hamilton said.

"My friend would figure out a way. There's an easy way to find out. Call my friend. He'll let you talk to Andrew so you'll know that I'm telling you the truth."

"Okay," Hamilton answered as he pulled his cell phone out of his pocket.

"What's the number?" Hamilton asked.

Hamilton punched the keys as Mohlar spoke the numbers. Then he held it to Mohlar's ear.

"Hello, Ken, this is Sam."

Before Mohlar could say anything more, Hamilton put the phone to his ear and said, "Hello, this is Randy Hamilton. I want to talk to my son."

"I'll let you talk to Andrew if I can talk to Mohlar."

Gray handed the phone to Andrew Hamilton and told him to be careful what he said to his father.

Randy said, " Andrew, are you all right?"

"Yes, Dad. Please make this man release me."

Gray took the phone and said, "Now let me talk to Mohlar."

Randy Hamilton was silent for a moment. Finally, he cupped his hand over the mouthpiece of the phone to muffle the sound and whispered to Mohlar, "Be careful what you say." Hamilton handed the phone to Scott to hold for Mohlar.

Mohlar, ignoring Randy Hamilton, said to Gray, "I'm in big trouble here. Hamilton had a guy beat me up. He hit me twice. Do the same to Andrew."

Upon hearing that, Hamilton took the club and hit Mohlar. The attack surprised Scott and he dropped the phone. Hamilton picked up the phone and said, "If you hit my son, I'll kill you."

Gray responded, "I've already hit Andrew twice. Listen carefully to me. Whenever you beat up Mohlar, I'll beat up Andrew; and I'll kill him if you kill Mohlar."

"I'll release Mohlar when you release Andrew," Hamilton said.

"First, you release Mohlar, and then I'll release Andrew," Gray replied.

"It appears we've reached an impasse," Hamilton replied.

"This reminds me of a John Wayne movie," Gray said. "In the movie the captors had each hostage walk from his captor to safety. That way the swap was made at the same time."

"That sounds good to me," Hamilton said. "I know of a short one-way street that is hardly ever traveled. I'll be on the north end of the street and will send Mohlar south. You can be on the south end of the street and send Andrew north. The street is called Olson Lane. It connects Treadwell and Barto. Let's make the swap at midnight."

"I gotta think about it for a couple of hours," Gray said. "When I've made a decision, I'll call you back."

After Hamilton gave Gray his phone number and ended his call, he said to Scott, "Keep an eye on Mohlar. I'm leaving now, but I'll return before Gray calls. I should be back in an hour."

Scott turned on the television and watched the movie *Seven Brides for Seven Brothers*.

When Mohlar realized that the movie was about people who were kidnapped, he started to become interested. He watched it intently, hoping to get an idea from the movie how he might escape.

In about two hours Hamilton's cell phone rang. He picked up the phone and said, "Hello, Hamilton here."

"Ken, here. I decided to make the swap, but here's how it's gonna happen. First, I'll be located on the north end of the street, and you'll be on the south end. Second, this will be done in the daylight, at noon or early afternoon."

"That's fine with me. Let's make the swap tomorrow at noon," Hamilton replied.

After Hamilton hung up the phone, he said to Mohlar, "I'm going to kill you and your friend sometime after I get my son back. I'm telling you now so it can weigh on your mind just when and how it will be done. Where's the money?" Hamilton asked Mohlar. "I intend to continue beating you until you answer my question."

"Ken will treat your son the same way you treat me, so you should drop the thought of beating me."

"All I have to do is keep you alive so I can swap you for Andrew. Your friend won't know how you were treated until after I have my son back. Unless you tell me where the money is, I'll have you beaten to the point where you'll wish you were dead. Scott, don't hit him in the head with the club. We don't want to risk killing him."

"I don't know where the money is," Mohlar insisted.

Scott growled like an animal as he picked up the club. He worked again with savage fury. Mohlar cringed with pain as the wooden club hit him. After twelve blows to the body, Scott put the club down. He put on a padded right-handed glove. He hit Mohlar in the head until he was unconscious.

FIFTEEN

Mohlar woke up the next morning tired. For much of the night he sat in pain on an uncomfortable chair tightly bound by ropes, watching Scott sleep.

The entire left side of Mohlar's face was black and sore. His head and back ached, and he wondered if he would be beaten again this morning.

Rosie Hamilton stared at Mohlar and lightly touched his bruised head with her fingers. He flinched and grimaced in pain. "Your face looks awful. Do you have a headache?"

"Yes," Mohlar answered curtly.

"If I put two tablespoons of liquid aspirin in a cup of orange juice, would you drink it?" she asked almost inaudibly.

"I'd like that," the detective answered.

Since his hands were still tied behind him, Mrs. Hamilton held the cup of orange juice so that he could drink it using a straw. She also spoon-fed him some cereal.

After Mohlar finished breakfast, he thought of a way of escaping. He said, "Would you untie my hands and feet so I can go to the bathroom?"

She reached down the V of her blouse and pulled out a short, flat compact black revolver. "You look surprised, Mr. Mohlar," she said smiling.

"I am," he said, realizing his plan of escaping was foiled. He didn't realize that she was armed. In fact, he didn't think it was possible for her to conceal a revolver under her blouse.

"I had this blouse and a holster specially made so I can conceal a revolver. Whenever I think I may be in danger, I carry a gun," she said.

She placed the revolver about ten feet from Mohlar and then untied his hands. He untied his feet while she picked up the revolver. His pain caused him to get up slowly and walk wearily. She pointed the revolver at him while he went into the bathroom.

"May I close the door so I may have some privacy?" Mohlar asked timidly.

"You can close the door."

Mohlar closed the door and searched for some way out, but could not find one. He ran cold water on a handkerchief, squeezed it, and held it on the left side of his face. While he was in the bathroom, he realized that the pain in his head had begun to subside.

When he came out of the bathroom, she pointed the revolver at him. After she made him drop the wet handkerchief and tied him up, she returned the revolver to beneath her blouse.

At exactly nine o'clock there was a knock at the door. Rosie Hamilton walked to the door, looked through the peephole, and pressed a button that released the lock. Mohlar was surprised to see Flood enter the room. Rosie said, "Mr. Hamilton is waiting for you in the room to your right."

———

Flood knocked at the door and Randy Hamilton told him to enter.

"I'm very pleased with the work you've been doing for me," Hamilton said. "That was a large delivery of drugs you brought in from the U.S. on Wednesday."

"Thanks for the generous payment for my work," Flood responded.

Hamilton looked Flood straight in the eye and said, "I'm the greatest criminal in Canada. Besides dealing in drugs, I run houses of prostitution and I sell protection. In the process of breaking many laws, I've made enemies. Sometimes I need to kill my enemies. I heard you'll do a hit if the price is right. There're two guys I want you to eliminate. What's your price?"

"Ten grand each. Who am I knocking off?"

"One is the man who is tied up in the other room. Here is a picture I took out of his wallet. His name is Sam Mohlar."

"You did the hard part by capturing him and tying him up. So all you want me to do is kill him?"

"It's not going to be that easy. His friend kidnapped my son, Andrew. In order to get Andrew back, I have to release Mohlar. The other man I want you to kill is the man who took Andrew. Here is a picture of him. As you can see from the back of the picture, his name is Ken Gray."

"Maybe I can shoot them both when the trade for Andrew is made."

"That's what I'm thinking. But Andrew must be safe before you shoot. If you can't shoot them at that time, maybe you can track them down later."

"When will the swap happen?"

"Today at noon. Meet me here at eleven."

After Flood left, Hamilton made several calls to friends to seal off Barto Street so Mohlar and Gray could not escape. Hamilton then joined his wife, who was still watching Mohlar.

Randy Hamilton, noticeably worried, whispered to his wife the details of his plan. Rosie Hamilton cried and yelled, "Do whatever you have to do to get my son back!"

At eleven Flood returned armed with a loaded rifle. He took two large dark blue bandanna handkerchiefs out of his pocket. He tied one over Mohlar's eyes. Mohlar was gagged with the other. Then Randy and Rosie Hamilton and Richard Flood escorted Mohlar out of the warehouse and walked toward a car.

Mohlar's pains faded as the fresh air revived him. The wonderful aroma of a nearby bakery refreshed him. The loud and constant roar of the falls energized him.

Flood opened the trunk of the Pontiac and forced Mohlar into it. Flood drove Mohlar and the Hamiltons to the south end of Olson. While they waited for Gray to arrive, they got Mohlar out of the trunk and put him into the back seat of the car. They took the bandanna off his eyes, but left the other bandanna in his mouth.

At noon Gray arrived armed with a rifle. He was wearing a mask so that Randy Hamilton and his gang would not get a good look at his face. Andrew Hamilton was tied and gagged in the back-seat of his car.

A few minutes later two cars arrived and parked behind Gray's car on Barto. Gray suspected that these cars belonged to Hamilton's friends and that they had arrived to prevent Mohlar and him from escaping.

Gray called Hamilton and asked, "Do you have Mohlar with you?"

"Yes. Do you have Andrew with you?"

"Yes. If you want him back, call off your goons in the two cars behind me."

A minute later, the two cars departed.

Gray continued talking to Hamilton. "Untie and ungag Mohlar and I will do likewise to Andrew. In exactly two minutes from when we stop talking, you send Mohlar my way and I'll send Andrew heading your way. And if I see you double-crossing me, I'll shoot Andrew in the back."

"Let's leave their hands tied," Hamilton responded.

"If you want your son back alive, you'll do as I say."

"Deal."

In the next two minutes Gray and Randy Hamilton untied and ungagged their captives. Exactly when Mohlar walked toward Gray, Andrew walked toward his parents. Gray's eyes were focused on Andrew Hamilton. He didn't notice the two cars returning to Barto Street. However, Mohlar did.

As Mohlar and Andrew Hamilton were walking, they were staring at each other. Mohlar prayed, *Lord, please give me the strength for what I'm about to do.*

When Mohlar was next to Andrew, he suddenly grabbed

Andrew, put him in a neck lock, and twisted him so his back was toward his parents.

Randy and Rosie Hamilton grabbed Flood as he was getting ready to shoot and said, "Don't shoot. You'll hit my son."

Rendering Andrew helpless in his arms, Mohlar pulled him toward Gray. Then Gray opened the back door of his car and Mohlar pushed Andrew in.

Randy Hamilton called his friends in the cars on Barto and ordered them to let Gray and Mohlar go because they had captured his son.

Unaware of Hamilton's phone call, Gray said, "Sam, grab the rifle. We may have to shoot our way out of here."

While Mohlar grabbed the rifle, Gray put the accelerator to the floor. As the car lunged forward, Andrew tried to open the door but it was locked. While Mohlar pushed him away from the door, he dropped his rifle. When Mohlar grabbed the rifle, Andrew unlocked the door, opened it, and jumped out. He landed just past the two cars on Barto Street.

The men in the cars started shooting at Gray's car. Mohlar and Gray heard the bullets hitting the car and shattering the back window. The two cars chased Gray's car down Barto Street. In his excitement, Mohlar shot back, but missed.

As Gray approached a traffic light, it turned red. He pushed the accelerator to the floor, sounded the horn, and hoped the intersection would be clear for them to pass through. After they got through the intersection, the traffic flow resumed. The cars chasing Gray's car slammed on their brakes and stopped at the intersection. The two detectives drove away unharmed.

When they returned to Mohlar's motel room, Gray said, "It looks like Randy Hamilton worked you over pretty good."

"He gave that pleasure to his assistant. I've never been beaten worse in my life than I was last night. Rosie Hamilton gave me some aspirin this morning that relieved the pain for a while. Now I'm hurting again." Mohlar walked to the bathroom, filled a cup with water, found a bottle of aspirin he had left on the counter, and took two of them. He turned to Gray and said, "Maybe that will help."

"Maybe a hot bath will lessen your pain."

"I'll take your advice. Ken, I owe my life to you. I can never repay you for what you did for me."

"I also owe my life to you 'cause if you wouldn't have grabbed Hamilton, we would not have escaped," Gray replied.

Then Mohlar said, "You'll have to be the one to contact Flood, because he'll recognize me. But I'm sure he didn't get a good look at you. You were too far away from him."

When Gray left, Mohlar turned on the bathroom water and undressed so there would be no delay before he slid into the soothing warm soapsuds. After soaking for an hour, the pain started to creep from his bruised body. Mohlar fell asleep and woke up pain free half an hour later.

SIXTEEN

Nine hours after Mohlar was rescued from the Hamiltons, Kay Townsend was playing gin rummy with her attractive sister, Jenny, who was two inches taller than Kay. Kay saw anger in her eighteen–year–old sister's blue eyes, and she knew it was because Jenny hadn't scored a point in the game. Kay drew a card from the stock and for the third consecutive hand said, "Gin."

After Jenny dealt the cards, she pulled her feet under her while sitting in a chair. She asked, "Is this guy you've been dating good looking?" The tone of her voice and her hard eyes indicated to Kay that she was trying to conceal her irritation.

Kay thought, *I wish she wouldn't take these card games so seriously. If I talk to her about Sam and Bible quizzing, she might calm down.*

"He's gorgeous. He has beautiful blue eyes and a baby face. Actually, he looks a lot like Tom Cruise. This sure is a mess you dealt me," Kay said while picking up the face-up card, the four of spades.

"It must be better than my hand," Jenny said as she picked up the king of spades, which Kay just discarded. "How did your Tuesday night date go with the Tom Cruise look-alike?"

"His name is Sam," Kay said with dreamy eyes. She hesitated for a few seconds and then chose to draw a card from the talon instead of taking Jenny's discard. "We really had a good time. After we finished dinner, we danced." Kay discarded the queen of clubs.

Jenny drew a card from the stock and said, "I didn't know you knew how to dance."

Kay's eyes brightened as she grabbed Jenny's discard, the ten of hearts, and said, "Any girl can dance the way Sam dances."

Jenny slid a card off the top of the stock, peeked at it, put it on the discard pile, and said, "That sounds so romantic. First dinner, then dancing."

Kay started to pick it up. She then changed her mind and picked up a card from the stock of cards. "It was great while it lasted," Kay said after discarding a card.

"What does that mean?" Jenny asked while picking up a card from the stock of cards. She discarded the seven of hearts.

As Kay was picking up the discarded card, she said, "Soon after we finished our first and only dance, Sam got a call from the Rochester police and had to leave right away. I felt like Lois Lane right after Clark Kent ducked out on her to turn into Superman."

With a look of careful contemplation, Kay discarded a card. Jenny knitted her eyes, and after a few seconds picked up a card from the stock. She slapped the eight of hearts on the discard pile in frustration, remembering the last card she had discarded was the seven of hearts. Without hesitation, Kay drew a card from the stock and said, "Are you going to help me coach the Bible quiz team this year?"

"That would be a big time commitment for me. Dad said I can start classes next month, and I'm afraid my studies will take a lot of my time," Jenny said while taking and discarding the same card from the stock.

"I think it would be nice if you gave something back to the quiz program," Kay said as she took a card from the stock. "After all, you were in teen quizzing for five years. Maybe you could call the quiz director, Mark, and see if he could use you at the monthly quiz tournaments. I don't think that would be a big time commitment, and I think you'd make an excellent quiz master."

Jenny squinted, took a card from the stock, and said, "I'd like to be a quiz master. I'll give him a call in a couple of weeks."

Jenny started to lay a card down and then she put it back into her hand. She looked at Kay and asked uncertainly, "What card are you looking for? I know you're looking for one of these two cards. I have a feeling the one I discard will be the one you're looking for." Finally, Jenny discarded the seven of spades.

"You're right," Kay said as she picked up the discarded card. "Gin."

"Don't you ever lose?" Jenny asked disgustedly as she laid down her cards. "I don't need to count points because I know you won the game. I thought you said I dealt you a bad hand."

"You did. I got everything I needed right away."

"You're the luckiest person I've ever known."

"I don't think it's all luck," Kay said as she gathered the cards together.

"Are you saying I don't know how to play gin rummy? You know you've been incredibly lucky tonight."

Jenny, you should've been able to figure out I could use the seven of spades, Kay thought. *Don't argue with her and try to calm her down.*

She replied, "I've been lucky tonight. Probably my luck will change soon and you'll start winning."

The telephone rang. The Townsend sisters stared at it; they usually didn't have calls after nine in the evening. Kay picked it up on the fourth ring.

A man on the other end asked, "May I speak with Kay Townsend?"

"Speaking," she answered.

"Do you know Samuel Mohlar?"

"Yes, I do. And who are you?"

"My name is Ronald Vaughn. I work at the Niagara Falls Community Hospital in Niagara Falls, Ontario. This evening a man was brought to the hospital. He was in a car accident and died a short time after arriving at the hospital. Based on the contents of his wallet, we believe him to be Samuel Mohlar. We found your name and telephone number in his wallet. Would you come to the hospital and identify the body?"

Kay was trembling so much she could barely speak. "Of course," she whispered, "I'll be right there. I know where the hospital is, but where should I go in the hospital?"

"If you go to the main entrance, I'll be there to meet you. Please give me a brief description of yourself."

Sobbing, Kay replied, "I have blue eyes, brown hair, and I'm five-foot-two inches tall. I'll be at the hospital soon wearing a red blouse and blue jeans."

"Miss Townsend, I understand how shocking this telephone call is to you. You'll need to brace yourself and bear up. This may be a very harrowing experience for you."

Kay hung up the phone and walked over to Jenny. "What happened, Kay? Who were you talking to?"

"A man by the name of Ronald Vaughn said that Sam Mohlar died in a car accident. He wants me to go to Niagara Falls, Ontario, and identify the body. Do you know where Dad is? I want him to go with me."

"He didn't say where he was going. He said he'd be home by eleven."

"I'm not waiting. Tell him where I'm going."

———

An hour later, Kay arrived at the Niagara Falls Community Hospital. She went to the main entrance and approached a short, heavy man. The man asked, "Are you Kay Townsend?"

"Yes, I am," she replied.

"They've moved the body to the morgue downtown. Please come with me to identify the body."

Soon a black van with very few windows pulled up. The man escorted her into the backseat of the van. After a few seconds, a tall man sat down in the backseat of the van so that Kay was sitting between the two men.

While traveling downtown, the short man asked, "Do you know Mohlar's phone number?"

Kay's eyes widened with fear. Her head was spinning. *What's going on here?* she thought. Finally she asked, "Why do you need to know his number?"

"We may have to notify his next of kin," the man answered.

"I'll tell you his number if I identify the dead man as Mohlar," she replied.

He gave an impatient gesture with his hands and shouted, "You'll tell me now!"

"Who are you? Why do you want to know Mohlar's phone number?" she asked.

"I want to call Mohlar and tell him that it'll cost him one hundred grand to keep you alive."

"I only met Mohlar last Monday. He doesn't know me well enough to pay anything for my safety. Besides, I doubt he even has one hundred thousand dollars."

Randy Hamilton grabbed Kay's purse, searched its contents, and found the card with Mohlar's name and phone number on it. He said to the driver of the van, "Pull over to the phone booth in front of Amy's Jewelry Store."

Hamilton called Mohlar and said, "Hello, this is Randy Hamilton. I'm with your friend, Kay Townsend. Do exactly what I say if you want her to live. Put one hundred thousand dollars cash in bills no larger than fifty into a bag. Take the money to the bridge on Treadwell Street on the west side of the city at noon tomorrow. This bridge is four blocks west of Olson Lane. You must go to the bridge alone. If anyone is with you, she'll die. Put the money under the bridge and on top of the concrete support at the east side of the bridge. Leave the area immediately and wait for my call. When I'm sure I have all the money, I'll call you and tell you where Kay is."

"You need to give me more time to get the money. Tomorrow is Sunday, and the banks are closed on Sunday."

"Deliver the money at noon on Monday."

"I insist on hearing her voice. I need to know she's all right before I bring you the money."

Hamilton motioned the tall man to bring her to the phone.

Before Hamilton gave her the phone, he told her exactly what to say.

Kay, trying to control her trembling, said, "Hello, Sam. This is Kay. I haven't been hurt yet. Please give him the money. I'm afraid of what he'll do to me."

"Kay, tell him I'll give him the money Monday at noon," Mohlar said and then hung up the phone.

Mohlar clenched his fist in anger. *It's one thing for Hamilton to take his rage out on a strong man like me, but Kay! What a heartless, inexcusable act of savagery to inflict on a small, innocent girl like her,"* he thought. *I'm going to have to ask Joe Townsend for the money. How can I break the news to him that Kay has been kidnapped and is being held for ransom? There's no other way around it. I'll just have to call him and tell him straight out what the situation is.*

After waiting a few seconds, he called Joe and said, "This is Sam Mohlar. I have some bad news. Kay was kidnapped, and the kidnapper, Randy Hamilton, is demanding one hundred thousand dollars for her release. I don't know what to do. I don't have that much money. Could you get me the money by Monday morning? Hopefully my friend and I can rescue her before Monday. I have an idea where she might be held, but in case I'm wrong, Monday at noon I'll have to give the money to this man."

With pain and indignation in his voice, Townsend replied, "Dr. Mohlar, I'm confused. My daughter Jenny just told me that Kay went to Canada to identify your body. Now I'm talking to someone I thought was dead. Not only am I surprised you're alive, but you want me to give you one hundred thousand dollars. If you want the money, I must talk to Kay. She has to verify what you just told me."

"You can't talk to her. Hamilton didn't give me his phone number. He told me he'd kill her if I didn't give him the money."

"What you've told me doesn't seem logical. How does he know you have a hundred thousand dollars? Even if he knows you have that much money, why would you give up your money to free a woman you hardly know?"

"It doesn't matter how logical it seems, the fact of the matter is this: If I don't give him the money, Kay will die. You have to trust me on this. I'll sign anything you want and I'll pay you back every cent if it comes to that. But please get the money in case I can't rescue her before noon on Monday."

"I'll get it, but I'll hang on to it until she's released. How do you want the money?"

"It has to be in cash in bills no larger than fifties. Hamilton told me I have to be alone when I bring the money or he'll kill Kay."

"I'll give you the money Monday morning," Townsend replied. "But I don't understand why anyone would kidnap my daughter."

"I'll explain what happened when I have more time," the detective said. "But right now I need to find Kay."

SEVENTEEN

Mohlar nervously sat on the edge of his bed. He interlocked his fingers and cracked his knuckles, then said to Gray, "I think Hamilton may be holding Kay in the same room where he held me. I don't know of any other place to look for her. Let's see if she's there."

"Do you know where the room is?"

"This morning, when I was led out of the room where I was being held, I heard the falls and smelled a bakery. There were similar sounds and odors at the white warehouse where I followed Flood Wednesday night. It's possible I was held at that warehouse on the south side of the city. It's likely that Kay is being held there. Get prepared to break into that warehouse."

Gray walked back to his room, gathered his tools, and laid them on his bed. He put a small wrench, a wire cutter, an awl, and two screwdrivers into the pockets of his shirt and slacks. He got into his car and picked up Mohlar.

———

Hamilton took Kay Townsend to the white warehouse on the south side of the city. With her hands tied together, he led her to the same room where he held Mohlar the day before. After he tied her to a chair, he turned to Scott and said, "Guard this girl tonight."

Smiling, Scott replied excitedly, "I'll take pleasure in watching her."

Hamilton chuckled and said, "All you have to do is look at her face to see that I gave you a pleasant job."

"It's hard to look at the face of a girl who has a figure like that," Scott replied.

Turning back to Kay, Hamilton said, "I sure hope your boyfriend comes up with the money. It would be a shame to waste someone as young and as beautiful as you."

"What good would it do to kill me?"

"Mohlar will know that I mean what I say. I'll continue to put pressure on him until he gives me the money."

Hamilton went to his private office. He pulled a cell phone from his pocket. "Hello, this is Randy Hamilton. Am I speaking to Richard Flood?"

"Yep."

"I think Sam Mohlar will be at the bridge on Treadwell at noon on Monday. Four blocks west of Olson Lane. One good shot could earn you ten grand. Let him put something on the concrete support under the bridge before you fire."

"Thanks for the tip. Soon after I shoot him, you can expect me to see you about getting paid."

After Hamilton left, Scott walked slowly in front of Kay and looked her over. Smiling, he said, "You sure are pretty." She did not respond.

He placed his right hand on the back of her head and his fingers entwined her hair. She shook her head, freeing herself from his touch. He put his left hand on her neck.

She yelled, "Take your hands off me!"

Scott took a swing at her with his open right hand and slapped her across her face. "Watch your lip, girl."

He raised his hand to take another swing at her when she begged, "Please don't hit me again."

"I need to teach you to respect your elders," Scott said, his hand still raised in a striking position.

"I'm sorry I snapped at you," she replied. "I should've asked you not to touch me."

He lowered his hand onto his shirt.

Her eyes were wide with terror as she watched him unbutton

his shirt. She sat white-faced and frozen as she said to herself, *Oh, Lord, what does this man intend to do to me? Please protect me from him.*

Scott took off his shirt and sat in a chair. Kay watched his every move in fear.

"It's hot tonight," Scott said as he walked over to the refrigerator, pulled out a can of beer, and opened it.

"Yes, it is," she replied.

Scott chugged down all the beer in the can with just a few gulps and tossed the empty can in the wastebasket. "I'm going to enjoy three or four cans of beer, and then I'll enjoy you."

"What do you mean, 'I'll enjoy you'? I'm not a can of beer."

"I think you're old enough to figure that out."

Scott got up, walked over to the refrigerator, and pulled out another can of beer. He pulled off the top as he walked over to the television and programmed the VCR to start recording a few minutes later.

"May I have a drink?" Kay asked.

"Do you like the game show 'Family Feud'?" Scott asked, ignoring her question.

"That's my favorite game show," Kay answered.

After drinking his second can of beer, he said, "I'm taping two shows of it. In an hour we'll watch them."

"Why don't we watch them now?"

"It'll be fun playing the game while watching it. After each question, I'll stop the VCR. Then I'll write down an answer and you'll tell me your answer. If your answer is more popular than mine, I'll give you a reward. A while ago you asked me for a drink. I'll let that be your first reward."

"If my answer is better than yours, I think my reward should be that you let me go."

"Stop your whining, girl, or I'll belt you," Scott replied, while opening his third can of beer. "I'll guarantee you that won't be a reward."

"Yes, sir. What if your answer is more popular than mine?" she asked.

"I'll decide an article of clothing for you to take off. The game ends and the real fun begins when you don't have any clothes on."

"I'm not going to play," she said.

"It doesn't matter whether or not you play the game, the end result will be the same. If you don't play the game, I'll rip your clothes off. But if you play the game, I'll give you some nice rewards."

"I'll tell your boss what you did to me."

"He won't care," he said while finishing his third can of beer. "His only concern is that you're here in the morning when he comes back."

"I'll play the game," she said.

"This beer really hits the spot," Scott said after he opened his fourth can of beer.

Kay didn't respond. As she watched him drink can after can of beer, she became more and more afraid of what he would do to her. Kay was surprised and happy to watch Scott close his eyes and fall asleep.

Thank you, Lord, for protecting me from Scott, Kay said to herself. *But Lord, I still need your protection. What will happen to me if Sam can't come up with one hundred thousand dollars? Please send Daddy here, Lord. I know he can save me, or maybe you could send Sam to help me out of here. But they don't know where I am.* Kay felt a pang in her heart as she thought that perhaps no one would be sent to save her.

Then Kay was amazed as many phrases from the Bible came to her mind:

> Even though I walk through the valley of the shadow of death, I will fear no evil, for you are with me.[1] You will not fear the terror of the night, nor the arrow that flies by day.[2]
> If you make the Most High your dwelling...then no harm will befall you, no disaster will come near your tent. For He will command His angels concerning you to guard you in all your ways.[3]

Kay lowered her head and prayed, *Lord, I know my life is in your hands. My enemy may think he's in control because he has weapons and I don't. Lord, I know that you're in control. I believe that you can deliver me from this danger. Even if you don't deliver me, that will be okay. Then I'll be with you forever.*

Suddenly, phrases spoken by Jesus came to her mind:

> Do not let your hearts be troubled. Trust in God; trust also in me. In my Father's house are many rooms; if it were not so, I would have told you. I am going to prepare a place for you. And if I go and prepare a place for you, I will come back and take you to be with me that you also may be where I am. You know the way to the place where I am going.[4]

She felt a peace come over her as she watched Scott sleep. She closed her eyes, hoping to fall asleep.

———

At 2:30 a.m. the two detectives arrived at the white warehouse. They found the doors locked.

Locks were never a problem for Gray. Without a key, he could unlock any door in less than a minute. Gray took out his tools and picked the lock. They walked down a hallway and found another locked door. Again Gray used his tools to unlock it.

Gray turned the knob with care so there was neither a rattle nor a click. He opened the door noiselessly and there she was! They saw Kay tied to a chair, her hands and feet bound. They could hear the low rumbles of Scott snoring, who was sitting next to her. Gray closed the door equally noiselessly.

Mohlar whispered to Gray, "I think we can get her out of here without Scott waking up. He was supposed to watch me last night, but slept soundly until morning."

Kay's eyes brightened as Mohlar and Gray quietly approached

her. Gray took a wrench from his pocket, raised it to strike Scott on the head, and glanced at his partner. Mohlar shook his head, and his lips shaped the silent word, "No." Gray returned the wrench to his pocket.

He cut the ropes around her ankles while Mohlar cut the ropes around her wrists. They were so intent on cutting the ropes that they didn't notice that Scott had opened his eyes. Mohlar looked into her deep blue eyes and whispered softly in her ear, "Darling Kay, you look so sweet."

Those words took her back to the restaurant. She recalled when he held her close and told her she was a sweet girl. The thought of him rescuing her revived her despite the many hours it had been since she had slept. She freed her hands and feet from the ropes and rose from her chair.

Scott quickly grabbed his club and swung it at Gray, hitting him in the back and knocking him to the floor. The impact of the strike on Gray's back caused Scott to lose his grip on the club. It fell loudly to the floor. Mohlar lunged at Scott, his knife outstretched. Scott avoided being struck by the knife and grabbed Mohlar's arm. Scott forced Mohlar to drop the knife.

Scott grabbed the knife. As Scott was coming toward Mohlar with the knife, Mohlar backed up toward Kay. Suddenly, Scott lunged toward Mohlar, but he was able to step aside, avoiding being struck by the knife. Kay saw she was about to be stabbed and tried to move out of the way, but she was too slow. The knife plunged into her abdomen. Scott pulled the knife out and turned once again to go after Mohlar.

Scott raised the knife with his right arm. When he started moving the knife down toward Mohlar, Mohlar grabbed Scott's right arm with both his hands. Mohlar was strong enough to stop the stabbing motion. Scott put his left hand on the handle of the knife. Both men pushed with equal force, resulting in no movement. After struggling for a few seconds, Scott was able to get the knife moving slowly toward Mohlar.

Gray saw Mohlar was in trouble. He stood up, ran over, and

grabbed Scott from behind. Gray put his two powerful hands around his neck. When he started to squeeze, Scott dropped the knife and grabbed Gray's fingers.

Gray said to Mohlar, "I got him under control. You take care of the girl."

Mohlar pulled off his shirt and ran to the bathroom. He soaked his shirt under the water tap and ran back to Kay. He placed the shirt on the wound in her stomach to stop the bleeding. Gray's hands were too powerful for Scott to loosen the hold on his neck. Scott couldn't get air. Finally, he lost consciousness.

While Gray tied up Scott, Mohlar picked up Scott's shirt that was still lying on a chair. He tied the shirt around Kay's waist.

When Gray finished tying up Scott, he helped Mohlar get Kay to her feet. They each took one of her arms and picked her up. As her legs weakened, she put her head on Mohlar's shoulder. She sighed and closed her eyes. As she lost consciousness, Scott regained his.

Mohlar and Gray carried her to the car. They placed her in the backseat of the car and Mohlar sat next to her.

"Do you know where the hospital is?" Mohlar asked as he buckled his seatbelt.

"I cruised by it yesterday," Gray said as he pushed the accelerator to the floor and drove as quickly as he could to the hospital. Fortunately, very few cars were on the streets that night. Gray did not even stop for red lights.

While Gray was driving, Mohlar dialed 911 and frantically said, "My name is Sam Mohlar. A girl has been stabbed. We'll be at the hospital in a few minutes, but I don't know where the emergency room is. I pray she can hang on until we get there. Let them know what's happened."

A woman answered, "I'll let the hospital know the situation. What direction are you heading?"

"North."

"As soon as you enter the south entrance of the hospital, you will see signs for the emergency room. Follow the signs."

"Okay," Mohlar replied.

When Gray stopped the car in front of the emergency room doors, the hospital staff took Kay and carried her into the hospital. While Gray told the hospital staff what happened, Mohlar called Joe Townsend.

"Joe, we found Kay. While we were trying to rescue her, she was stabbed. We are at the Niagara Falls Community Hospital."

"Is she going to live?" Townsend asked in a quivering voice.

"We won't know until we talk to the doctor."

"I'll be at the hospital soon."

"Joe, Hamilton is clearly a threat to you and your family. He knows that he can get to me through you. I suggest that you evacuate your house immediately and find a place where you will be safe."

"I guarantee you, my first priority will be to protect my family. As soon as I know they're safe, I'll be at the hospital."

Fifteen minutes later a doctor came out to talk to them.

"We've just given Miss Townsend a blood transfusion. They're taking her to surgery now."

"What are her chances of survival?" Mohlar inquired.

The doctor frowned and slowly shook his head. "Not good, I'm afraid, not good. She has suffered a severe wound, but she's young and has obviously kept herself in good physical condition. It's good that you guys got her here as quickly as you did. If you would've taken five minutes longer, she would've been dead on arrival—"

"—I'm sorry to interrupt, but I have questions for the men who brought in the girl who was stabbed. I'm Lieutenant Cobb; I'm with the Niagara Falls Police Department."

"I'm Sam Mohlar, and this is my friend Ken Gray. Miss Townsend was stabbed and we brought her to the hospital," Mohlar said in a robotic voice. So much had happened that he couldn't let his emotions take control.

"What happened?" Cobb said while pulling a notepad and pen from his shirt pocket.

"We got in a fight with Henry Scott. He accidentally stabbed her."

"Do you think I'll be able to talk to her?" Cobb asked.

"The doctor just told us that her chances aren't good. She's in surgery now," Mohlar said in a monotone voice.

"Mr. Mohlar, what's your relationship with Miss Townsend?" Cobb asked with a suspicious look in his eyes.

"She's my friend."

"Mr. Gray, what's your relationship with Miss Townsend?"

"She's a friend of my friend, Sam."

Cobb paused and stared at Mohlar's head. "Mr. Mohlar, how did you get all those bruises on your face?"

"Scott repeatedly hit me in the head."

"You must be in a great deal of pain."

"It's not as bad as it looks. I don't have any pain unless I touch it."

"Maybe Townsend hit you in the head," Cobb suggested. "Maybe you got so mad at her, you stabbed her. Then you became sorry you stabbed her and you asked Mr. Gray to help you bring her to the hospital."

While dialing his cell phone, Mohlar said, "I work for the Rochester Police Department in the U.S.A. I just dialed their number. Ask to speak to Lieutenant Elwood Luff. He'll tell you that I wouldn't stab anyone."

Cobb took the phone and said, "May I speak to Lieutenant Elwood Luff?"

"Lieutenant Luff speaking."

"I'm Lieutenant Cobb of the Niagara Falls Ontario Police Department. Sam Mohlar says he works for the Rochester Police Department. Is that true?"

"That's true. We've worked together on many homicide cases."

"It appears that Mohlar has been in a fight; there are many bruises on his face. He brought a girl to a hospital with a knife wound, and I think he fought with this girl and stabbed her."

"What did Mohlar say happened?"

"He said Henry Scott stabbed her."

"If Mohlar said that Scott stabbed her, then I believe that's what happened. I trust Mohlar without reservation."

"Thanks for your help."

Cobb handed Mohlar his cell phone, looked him straight in the eye, and said, "I believe you're telling me the truth. Can you tell me anything else about what happened?"

Mohlar answered, "A man by the name of Randy Hamilton kidnapped Miss Townsend and demanded ransom for her release. Mr. Gray and I found her, but Scott was guarding her. We got in a fight with Scott, and he accidentally stabbed her."

"Hamilton is the most powerful man in Niagara Falls," Cobb replied. "He's very well liked here because his casino employs many people. Other businesses thrive here because of his casino. If we were to arrest him, he'd never be convicted of a crime. He's the richest man in the city and would hire the best lawyers. Actually, he's bugged the police for years. We've arrested him many times before, and he has had many trials. He always had good alibis. I think Hamilton has good liars who are willing to speak up for him. I don't have any more questions now. You can leave whenever you want."

Mohlar and Gray agreed to stay until Kay's father arrived. As soon as he arrived, they returned to their motel rooms, completely exhausted.

EIGHTEEN

Early the next morning Randy and Andrew Hamilton went to their office. When they opened the door, they were surprised to see Scott tied up. They quickly cut the rope, releasing Scott's hands and feet.

"What happened?" Randy asked.

"Mohlar and someone else jumped me and released the girl. I took away Mohlar's knife. I got in a fight with him, and I accidentally stabbed the girl. The other guy grabbed me from behind and almost choked me to death. Then everything went black. When I came to, they were carrying the girl away and I was tied to this chair."

"Is she dead?" Andrew asked.

"I don't know."

———

Soon after Mohlar woke up that morning, he went out into the bright July sun and walked slowly over to Gray's motel room. He found Gray eating cereal and bagels.

"If you want to go to the hospital, I can keep an eye on Flood," Gray said while pouring a cup of orange juice. "Call me sometime and let me know how she's doing."

"Thanks for the offer. Let me know of any developments here."

———

While Randy Hamilton was talking to Scott, Andrew Hamilton slipped out of the office and called Flood. "How much would a tip to find Gray and Mohlar be worth to you?" Andrew asked in a voice that was barely audible.

"I'll give you a C-note for each one you help me find. But if your tip doesn't help me find either of them, I'll pay you nothing."

"Fine. I think you'll find them in the waiting room of the Emergency Room or the Intensive Care Unit of the hospital in the city."

"Which hospital in the city?"

"Niagara Falls Community Hospital. It's the only hospital in the city."

Flood wasn't sure how he was going to kill them, so he put a revolver, billy club, knife, and a vial of poison into his pockets. He wanted to be prepared for any opportunity that might come his way.

———

When Mohlar arrived at the waiting room of the Intensive Care Unit, he saw Joe Townsend playing solitaire. The only other person in the room was reading a magazine. Mohlar approached Townsend and said, "Joe, is Kay still unconscious?"

"They let me see her about twenty minutes ago, and she was still unconscious. Every hour they allow one visitor at a time and then for only five minutes. You may go in the next time. Why is this man, Hamilton, after you? Why did he kidnap my daughter?"

Mohlar explained the bag of money and Hamilton's obsession with getting back the missing one hundred thousand dollars. The detective said, "Hamilton thought he could recover the missing money by kidnapping Kay and holding her for ransom. I feel awful about what happened to Kay."

Townsend slammed his fist on the card table as he yelled, "My daughter may lose her life because of you. How could you let this happen?"

Mohlar lowered his head in shame. In a voice that was barely audible he said, "I know it's my fault. If I hadn't moved, Kay wouldn't have been stabbed. At the time, all I could think of was getting out of the way of that knife. I didn't realize that would mean—"

"No, no; it's not your fault," Townsend interrupted. "You were rescuing my daughter. I'm just so upset right now. Hamilton's the one at fault. He's the one who is putting my daughter through all of this."

Mohlar wiped a tear from his cheek and tried to think of a way to help Joe Townsend through the terrible time. "Would you like to play gin rummy?" Mohlar asked, trying to come up with a pleasant way of passing time.

Townsend agreed, and after cutting the deck they determined that Townsend would deal first. It was obvious to Mohlar that Townsend was an experienced card player. The way he shuffled and dealt the cards reminded Mohlar of casino dealers. Hour after hour they played cards while waiting to hear a report from the doctor.

Each hour, on the hour, Mohlar and Townsend alternately went into the Intensive Care Unit to see Kay. They watched her sleep, talked to her without knowing if she heard or understood anything that they said, and prayed with her before the end of the five minutes.

While Townsend was visiting his daughter, Mohlar called Gray. "Any sign of Flood today?"

"Our man is on the move and I'm right behind him. How is Kay doing?"

"She's doing about the same. She still hasn't regained consciousness."

"I'll keep you posted on what Flood is doing," Gray said.

"The hospital prohibits incoming cell phone calls. I'll call you often."

A few minutes later Mohlar called his partner. Gray said, "I'm afraid I'm going to lose Flood. I'm three cars behind him. I can't close the gap 'cause the traffic is heavy."

At 2:15 a doctor walked up to Mohlar and Townsend and said, "In a few hours we'll move Miss Townsend to a larger hospital in

St. Catherines, which is only twenty miles away. They'll be better able to take care of her there."

"I want my daughter to be wherever she'll receive the best care. I trust your judgment on this."

After the doctor left, Mohlar called Gray.

"I lost Flood in traffic," Gray said. "He may have been heading for the casino. I'll check it out."

"If he's not there, just go back to the motel. Sometime he'll return to his room."

When Mohlar hung up the phone, Flood arrived at the hospital. In a short time he found Mohlar and Townsend. He positioned himself so he was back-to-back with Mohlar. Townsend could only see the back of his head. From that position Flood could hear them but neither of them could see his face. He thought he would just wait for Mohlar to be alone and then he would kill him.

"Is your family safe?"

"They're at my sister Bonnie's house," Townsend answered. "My sister is working now, but I think they're safe. She said we could stay there until we get a chance to move into an apartment."

Mohlar and Townsend began to talk of the latest plays. Mohlar found Townsend's judgments were sound and his criticisms insightful. Their conversation led to books and then to world politics. He found Townsend to be a well informed, intelligent man.

"Do your wife and kids expect you home at any particular time tonight?" Mohlar asked.

"My wife died about three years ago in a car accident. My daughter Jenny said she'd take care of my son, Billy, until I came home. I told her I didn't know when I'd come home, but I would call them often. I've been calling them every other hour while you've been in to see Kay."

"I'm sorry to hear that your wife died."

"Her death was a tremendous blow to me, both emotionally and financially. Her income was almost double my income. She was a teacher and I'm a pastor. When she died, we didn't have enough money to live on."

"Did you have any life insurance?"

"We thought life insurance to be a poor investment, so we had none. I may have exaggerated my situation. We had enough money for our basic needs, but we couldn't live as we were accustomed to living."

"Is that why Kay worked instead of going to college?"

"Kay was tremendous. She saw her family needed help, so she postponed her education to support the family. I felt bad about that, because Kay liked school and was a very diligent student. In fact, she was the valedictorian of her class."

"I could tell she was intelligent the first time I met her."

"I hated to break up my baseball card collection. When you expressed interest in buying some of my cards, I saw an opportunity to give my children a college education. I should've sold those cards three years ago, so Kay could've attended college the fall after she graduated from high school. I also hated selling my wife's antique furniture because I knew how much she loved that furniture. But as we needed money, I sold the furniture. I only have a few pieces left."

"Now I understand why you have a unique mixture of antique and modern furniture in your house. A few days ago I had a delicious pizza at Deano's Pizzeria. I'm going to call them for a pizza to be delivered here. Would you help me eat it?"

"No thanks," Townsend answered. "I don't want anything to eat, but you go ahead and order what you want."

While Townsend shuffled and dealt the cards for a hand of gin rummy, Mohlar phoned the pizzeria.

"Is this Deano's Pizzeria?"

"Yes."

"My name is Sam Mohlar. I want to order a small pizza with pepperoni, onions, double cheese, and double mushrooms. I also want a large root beer. Please deliver my order to the waiting room of the Intensive Care Unit at the Niagara Falls Community Hospital."

"Your order comes to eight dollars. We'll be there in about forty-five minutes."

When Flood overheard him place his order, he saw his opportunity to kill Mohlar. He went to wait for the pizza deliveryman to arrive at the hospital.

At three o'clock it was Mohlar's turn to go into Kay's room. He said, "Kay, I don't know if you can hear me, but I want to tell you I love you. I love you more than I've loved any other person in my life."

She opened her eyes for just a second and then closed them. She was sleeping.

Could this be a sign that she was coming out of her coma? Mohlar thought. *My heavenly Father, I thank you for what I just saw. I pray that you will continue to help Kay become conscious and heal her wounds. I pray this in the precious name of Your Son, Jesus. Amen.*

When he told Joe about what had just happened, they both thanked God that Kay was recovering. About fifteen minutes later a doctor updated them on her condition.

"Miss Townsend has gained consciousness. All her vital signs have improved; I expect her to have a full recovery."

After the doctor left, Joe Townsend asked, "What kind of work are you in, Sam?"

"I'm a private detective. I bought the baseball cards from you because the man we are trying to locate is a collector. We'll use the cards as bait for a trap for him."

"Why did you become a private detective? I would think that with your educational background you could find a well-paying job that is both safe and secure."

"Shortly after I earned my Ph.D., my father was murdered," Mohlar said in a sad voice. "Since he was a judge in Rochester, the police had many suspects. Many people hated him because he usually gave convicted criminals the maximum sentence.

"I worked closely with the Rochester Police Department in solving the case. All the information we received was pooled; we didn't keep any knowledge to ourselves. However, I did keep deductions and impressions to myself until I'd developed a theory consistent with the facts. I suggested a theory to Lieutenant Luff, a homicide detective in the police force. The theory turned out to be true and led to the arrest and conviction of the woman who murdered my father."

"What was your theory?"

"My theory was based on a clue at the crime scene that was overlooked by everyone but me. That clue was found on a dollar bill. Joe, take a dollar bill out of your wallet and look it over. Find things on the bill that suggests a woman or the military."

Townsend took a dollar bill out of his wallet and looked it over for a minute. "George Washington was a general," Townsend said.

"Do you see anything else?"

"Nothing else," Townsend answered.

"There was a dollar bill and a pen near my father's body. Do you see the phrase, 'This note is legal tender for all debts public and private' on the bill?"

"The word 'private' suggests to me a private in the army," Townsend answered.

"Very good. My theory was this: When my father was shot, he didn't die immediately. In the last few seconds of his life, he underlined 'gal' of 'legal' and the word 'private' to point to his killer. Based on this clue, I suggested to Lieutenant Luff that my father's murderer was a woman who was a private in the military. After we investigated military units near Rochester, we found a woman in the army who had a connection with my father. Two months later we had enough evidence to arrest her."

"Why did she kill him?"

"I'm ashamed to say they were having an affair. When he wanted to end it, she killed him."

Mohlar was uncomfortable talking about his father's marital unfaithfulness. Desiring to change the subject, Mohlar said, "Let me return to your original question of why I became a private detective. Luff wanted me to work in his homicide division of the police department; he said that I have unusual powers of observation and deduction. He said that an investigation of a homicide is often a scientific matter involving precise mathematical calculations. He thought that with my academic background I'd be an asset to the division. Although I liked Luff and I liked the work, I declined his offer because I didn't want to work under someone else.

"A month later I set up a private investigation business with my friend, Ken Gray. Soon after that I got a call from Lieutenant Luff because he wanted me to help him with a murder investigation. The victim had a letter in his pocket, but the message in the letter was written in code. Since Luff knew I was a mathematician, he thought I might be able to decode the message. It was a simple code—just replace each letter in the message with the next letter in the alphabet, with 'z' being replaced by 'a.' It took me two hours to decode the message. After the letter was decoded, the Rochester police arrested a man who was later convicted of the murder. Since that investigation, Luff has called me to investigate many other homicides."

"Do police departments usually work with private detectives to solve homicide cases?"

"Private detectives are legally bound to report to the police any information they uncover that is relevant to a crime. Sometimes when that happens, the police and the private detectives find themselves working together to solve crimes. I know several private detectives who have helped the cops solve homicide cases. Have you heard about the Dean Milo murder case in the Midwest?"

"Wasn't he the head of the company that sold discount beauty products to barbershops and beauty salons?"

"That was Dean Milo. After he was murdered, his widow hired a private detective named Bill Dear to find the killer. The police had a suspect in mind, Barry Boyd, but Boyd wouldn't talk. So Dear did something the police couldn't do—he hounded Boyd. Wherever Boyd went, Dear would be close behind. Dear was constantly harassing Boyd. He told Boyd he wouldn't let up until the police arrested him.

"The police and Dear worked together with the common purpose of getting enough evidence to arrest Boyd. When the police finally arrested Boyd, he told them who was behind Dean Milo's murder."

"So who killed Dean Milo?"

"Boyd told the police that Dean's brother, Fred, hired a hit man to kill Dean. A few months later, Bill Dear found the hit man, David Harden. Harden collaborated Boyd's story that Fred hired him to kill his brother. Just like Bill Dear, I work with the police on homicide cases."

The man who was in the waiting room put his magazine down. He walked over to Mohlar and Townsend and asked, "Where is the cafeteria?"

"On the ground floor," Mohlar answered. "I ordered a pizza that should be here soon. If you'd like, I'll share it with you."

The man asked, "Will there be enough for three of us?"

"My friend doesn't want any. There will be more than I can eat."

"I like pizza," the man said. "But I insist on paying for my share."

The man walked back to his chair and continued to read his magazine.

Fifteen minutes later the detective said to Townsend, "I wish I hadn't ordered that pizza. I'm too upset to eat."

"Maybe the other guy will want the whole pizza," Townsend replied.

Flood saw the pizza delivery car as soon as it pulled into the parking lot. As the deliveryman parked the car near the entrance to the hospital, Flood walked toward the car. The deliveryman walked around the front of the car and opened the passenger door. Before he had a chance to pick up the pizza and drink, Flood came up behind him and hit him so hard with a club that he knocked the man unconscious. Fortunately for Flood, no one saw him attack the man.

Flood picked up the pizza and root beer and went into the hospital. He entered a restroom and went into the last stall. He then opened the vial of poison, emptied it into the root beer and flushed the vial away. After he left the restroom, he found an elevator.

He took the elevator to the third floor. When he walked out of the elevator, he saw a young man at a water fountain. While he was pointing to the waiting room of the Intensive Care Unit, he said, "See the two men playing cards in the waiting room?"

"Yes."

"Please give this pizza and drink to the man with the beard," he said and handed the young man a twenty-dollar bill. "His name is Sam Mohlar. You can keep the money he pays you for the delivery."

"Sure. Thanks, mister."

Flood waited by the water cooler as the young man walked into the waiting room and approached Mohlar. The young man said, "Are you Sam Mohlar?"

"Yes," he said as he was rising out of his chair.

"Here is your pizza delivery."

Mohlar paid for the delivery and gave the young man a generous tip. The young man smiled and put the money in his pocket as he left the room.

The man who agreed to share the pizza with Mohlar walked up to him and said, "How much do I owe you for my share of the pizza? Don't forget to include the tip."

"Your share is five dollars, but you can take all the pizza and drink," Mohlar answered. "I don't feel like eating anything."

The man was obviously hungry, because he ate the pizza in a hurry; however, he only drank about half the soda. About an hour after he finished the pizza, he stood up and started walking toward the magazine rack. After he took three steps, he started to stagger.

"Good grief, what happened to the guy who ate your pizza?" Townsend said as he watched the man suffer a violent spasm that threw him to the floor. He tried to get to his feet and started to rise, but suffered another spasm that made him collapse again.

When Flood saw the man stagger and fall to the floor, he left.

"Get a doctor here right away," Mohlar said to Townsend as he rushed toward the man. The man's arms were moving back and forth as he was struggling to live a few moments longer. His face was turning blue. In desperation Mohlar gave him mouth-to-mouth resuscitation. After a few minutes the man's eyes stared, without seeing.

Soon a doctor arrived and checked for vital signs. "He's dead," the doctor said.

"Maybe the drink should be checked since he drank almost half a cup of soda," Mohlar suggested. "He ate pizza an hour ago."

"I'll send the drink to the lab in the hospital and have a chemical analysis done on it," the doctor said as he covered the body with a blanket. "Did you know this man?"

"Not really," Mohlar answered. "I just met him today. I briefly spoke with him twice."

Thirty minutes later a homicide detective entered the waiting room where Mohlar and Townsend were playing gin rummy. "I am Lieutenant Cobb, and I'm investigating the murder of Ronald Cheesright."

"Are you sure he was murdered?" Townsend asked as he rose to his feet. Mohlar remained sitting.

"The soda he was drinking had a large concentration of potassium cyanide," the lieutenant said. "Mr. Mohlar, I remember meeting you last night."

"We should meet under more pleasant circumstances," Mohlar suggested.

"Did either of you know Mr. Cheesright?"

"No," they both answered.

"To whom was this pizza and drink delivered?" Cobb asked as he took a notepad and pen out of his pocket.

Mohlar answered, "I ordered a pizza and drink, and it was delivered to me here about one and a half hours ago."

"Where did you order the pizza from?"

"Deano's Pizzeria."

"Why didn't you eat the pizza?"

"I didn't feel like eating. Mr. Cheesright was hungry, so I gave him the pizza and drink."

"Can you describe the delivery man?"

"I'd say he was between twenty and twenty-five, weighing between one hundred-forty and one hundred-sixty pounds, and about five-foot-seven to five-foot-ten inches tall," Mohlar said as he rose to his feet. "He had brown eyes and dark brown hair."

"Did he have any distinctive facial features?"

"He had a small mole under his right eye."

After the lieutenant left, Mohlar said to Townsend, "That innocent man died instead of me. Your daughter was stabbed because she knew me. Maybe I shouldn't be around you or your family."

"The police should've given us more protection than they did," Townsend responded. "I'll talk to Lieutenant Cobb and see if he can get us more protection while we are here and when we get to St. Catherines. Considering what has happened the last two days, I think they'll protect us better. Please wait with me tomorrow in the St. Catherines hospital. Waiting is easier when you're with me."

"We're fortunate that they're moving Kay to another hospital. The longer we stay at this hospital, the more danger we are in. I suggest we better leave now and meet tomorrow in St. Catherines."

NINETEEN

Gray woke just after dawn the next morning. He rose and looked out at the street, which was quiet and peaceful. An hour later, he left his motel room and looked at the beautiful and magnificent falls that was in the form of a horseshoe. A bright, clear rainbow shone through the mist of the falls. *This is one of the most beautiful sights in the whole world, and I haven't even taken the time to enjoy it,* he thought.

As Gray walked north along the street, heading for the cafe where he agreed to meet Mohlar for breakfast, the second set of falls became visible—the falls on the American side—a beautiful sight as well. More mist was around the second falls. *How high are these falls? How many gallons of water fall over these falls per minute? Did someone create these falls?* He had many questions, but knew the answers to none of them.

An hour later Mohlar woke up. The windows of his motel room were open; the air was cool and he was comfortable. He started the day with a prayer of thanksgiving to God for his protection the day before. After he showered, shaved, and dressed, he walked to the cafe where Gray was waiting.

They each ordered a large orange juice with ice while they looked over the menu. After a few minutes, Mohlar finished his drink and rattled the ice. When a waiter who was passing by heard this, he stopped and took their orders.

After Mohlar updated his partner on the condition of Kay Townsend, he said, "It appears that yesterday someone tried to poison me while I was at the Niagara Falls Community Hospital. I'm guessing Flood put poison in my drink."

"I think Hamilton tried to poison you. After all, we know he has a motive to kill you. Why do you suspect Flood?"

"When I was tied up in Hamilton's office, Flood came into the room and then went into another room for a private conversation with Hamilton. A few minutes later, Hamilton came out and told me he was going to kill us both. I'm thinking that Hamilton hired Flood to kill us."

Gray thought for a few seconds and said, "Maybe Flood was hired to kill Krista Clark. That would explain where the money came from that he sent to his mother."

"Maybe you're right," Mohlar said slowly and thoughtfully. "That also might explain how he unlocked the door. Whoever hired him may have given him a key to the door."

Mohlar finished his second glass of orange juice and picked up both checks. The detectives walked out the front door of the cafe and stood for a moment in the sunshine, inhaling the fresh morning air. Mohlar and Gray parted. Mohlar went to St. Catherines and Gray returned to his motel room, again enjoying the beauty of the area.

At ten o'clock Flood walked out of his motel room. He climbed into his car, started it, and swung into traffic. Gray eased his car into motion with two cars between his car and Flood's. The traffic was bumper to bumper. That was fine with Gray. He was always able to keep Flood's car in view.

Gray followed Flood to the convention hall that was hosting a sports card show.

———

Mohlar arrived at the St. Catherines General Hospital about two hours before noon. When Mohlar entered Kay Townsend's private room, he found her sleeping and her father reading a magazine.

"How is Kay doing?" Mohlar whispered.

"I haven't had a chance to talk to her this morning. She has been sleeping ever since I got here."

Joe Townsend walked over to the window in the room and looked at the city. For the next half hour, Mohlar and Joe Townsend didn't talk much. Each of them found the other's silence restful.

At 10:30, a short white-haired nurse entered the room and said, "Good morning, gentlemen. I need to give Miss Townsend a sleeping pill."

"She doesn't need one," Joe replied. "She's sleeping."

"I'm a trained nurse, and I know it's important to wake her up and give her this sleeping pill."

"Dr. Mohlar, don't you think it's unusual to wake a lady up to give her a sleeping pill?" Townsend asked as he cracked a smile.

"It's not only unusual, I think it's ridiculous."

"I'm sorry; I didn't know you were a doctor. I'm afraid I'll be in trouble if I don't give her this pill; her doctor ordered me to give it to her."

"I'm a doctor, but not a medical doctor. You should follow the orders the doctor gave you."

———

Gray followed Flood through the doors of the convention hall. When a car backfired, Flood stopped. As he turned abruptly and looked over his shoulder at the car, Gray put his camera in front of his face pretending to take a picture. Flood was oblivious to Gray's presence.

Once inside the convention hall, Flood wandered from vendor to vendor, occasionally buying baseball cards. When Flood took some time talking to one of the vendors, Gray walked over to a nearby table and feigned interest in the cards on the table. Gray overheard Flood asking, "Have any cards of baseball players from the 1950s?"

"I don't have any cards that old anymore," the vendor answered.

Gray recognized this as a great opportunity to set a bait. He stepped forward and said, "I'm sorry to have listened in on your conversation, but I have some cards from the 1950s that I'm willing to sell."

Flood turned and smiled broadly because he recognized Gray from the picture he saw a few days ago. With eyes wide and bright, he asked, "What cards do you have?"

As Gray pulled out a baseball card from his shirt pocket, he said, "This card is the most valuable card I got. It's Mickey Mantle's rookie card. I also have cards of Willie Mays, Yogi Berra, Ted Williams, and Stan Musial."

Flood took the Mantle card and examined it. "Willing to sell this card?"

"Yes, if the price is right. I need to warn you that this card alone will cost you many thousands of dollars."

"I know this is a very valuable card. Are you also willing to sell the Mays, Berra, Williams, and Musial cards?"

"Yes, I'm willing to sell those cards, too, but I don't have them with me," Gray answered.

"Could you bring me those cards later today?"

"I live in the States," Gray responded as he put the Mantle card back into his shirt pocket. "I was planning on staying in Canada for the rest of the day. If you stop by my apartment tomorrow, I'll show you all my old, rare cards."

"I'd prefer that you bring your cards to my house. My name is Joseph Masters. I live at 395 Kitty Avenue in Buffalo. If you come to my house at 8:30 tomorrow morning, I'll look at your cards. I'll definitely make you an offer on the Mickey Mantle rookie card," Flood said.

"My name is Michael Streeter. I'll be at your place tomorrow morning with my baseball cards," Gray replied.

———

After the nurse woke Kay up and gave her a sleeping pill, she saw Mohlar and said, "You saved me. You and your companion saved me." She held out her hands to him. As he took them, he could see tears in her eyes. "I was afraid that huge man was going to hurt me or kill me."

"That man's name is Scott," Mohlar said while he was still hanging onto her hands. "Did he hurt you before we found you?"

"No, but I didn't know what he'd do to me if you couldn't get the money. In fact, I didn't think you had that much money."

"I was going to withdraw the money from the bank the next morning," her father said.

"Who is the man who kidnapped me?"

"This is the information I've found on him," the detective answered. "His name is Randy Hamilton. He's worth about fifty million dollars and keeps his hands on every penny of it. People think he obtained his wealth peddling illegal drugs. The drugs come into Canada from the U.S.A. at the border crossings in Niagara Falls and Buffalo. He buys the drugs that get through customs and then sells them for an enormous profit. The Ontario government has brought him to trial several times on drug trafficking charges, but each time he has been acquitted.

"Eight years ago he funded the construction of a casino in Niagara Falls, Ontario. The gaming business has been very profitable for him. He's married and has one child, a son, who is twenty-two. He's a devoted family man who viciously lashes out at anyone who harms his family. Not only am I an object of his wrath, but also anyone I know."

"Why does he want to hurt you?" she asked.

"The man who was with me when we freed you from Scott is my friend Ken. When he saw I was in danger from Hamilton, Ken kidnapped his son. When Ken heard that Scott was beating me, he beat up Hamilton's son. Hamilton was angry. He's used to throwing his weight around and watching everyone knuckle under his power. He was in the unusual position of having to work out a deal for the release of his son. He told me to my face that he was going to kill both Ken and me."

"Your friend Ken is an incredibly strong man," Kay said. "When I saw Scott hit him with a club, I thought he'd never get up. I was surprised and happy to see him soon stand up and grab Scott around the neck."

While she was talking, her doctor walked into the room. "Miss Townsend, you're rapidly recovering from your wound. I expect you'll soon be released from the hospital."

"What do you mean by 'soon'?" Kay asked.

"Three to five days," the doctor replied.

———

When Gray left the convention center, it was becoming dark. Dark clouds were blocking the sun out. A sprinkling of rain spattered against the windshield of his car when he was halfway between the convention center and his motel. By the time he reached the motel, the rain was coming down in torrents. Bolts of lightning zigzagged across the sky and were soon followed by deafening clashes of thunder.

Mohlar returned to his motel room shortly before Gray arrived and it started raining.

When Gray entered Mohlar's room, Mohlar asked, "Were you able to contact Flood today?"

"Yeah, I set up an appointment with him for 8:30 tomorrow morning at his house. He wants to see our baseball cards, particularly the cards from the 1950s."

"Good work, Ken. While you're showing him the baseball cards, mention to him that you have a friend who also has cards from the 1950s. Tell him that you'll call to see if it's okay for you both to visit him. When you come to my apartment and I open the door, quickly move away from him because I'll have a revolver pointed at him."

"That sounds like a good plan."

"Sam, do you remember when we were in high school, your father took us each summer to see a Yankees game? That was the highlight of my summer."

"Dad wanted you to go with us, not only because you were my friend, but because he knew how much you liked the Yankees."

Gray asked, "Do you think after we finish our job tomorrow, we could take a vacation? Let's go to New York City. The Yankees will be home for the next week. We could go to three or four ballgames. Maybe we could see a Broadway play while we're there."

"Let's do that, Ken. When we leave New York City, we could travel along the Hudson River and visit FDR's home in Hyde Park."

"On our way to Hyde Park, we could visit the U.S. Military Academy at West Point," Gray said.

"I don't want to leave until after Kay is well enough to be released from the hospital."

"How is Kay doing today?"

"She's doing much better. They have moved her out of ICU and put her into her own room. I want to see her early tomorrow before I go to my apartment in Buffalo. If you'd like, you can stay at my apartment tonight."

"That sounds good. Just make sure you get to your apartment no later than 8:40. When I call, I want you to be there."

"I'll give Clark a call. He'll want to be at my apartment when Flood arrives. If you wake up and leave early in the morning, put the key under the doormat so Clark can get in the apartment. He might get there before me."

Mohlar called Clark and said, "We've made contact with Flood. He lives at 395 Kitty Avenue in Buffalo. I expect tomorrow morning that Flood and Gray will arrive at my apartment between nine and eleven. Do you still want to meet with Flood before we turn him over to the police?"

"I'd like to see him tomorrow morning, but I may not be able to make it. If I'm not there, please proceed with your plans without me."

"If you arrive at my apartment and no one is there, you'll find my key under the doormat. Just let yourself in and make yourself at home."

After Mohlar hung up the phone, he asked, "How about our nightly game of cards?"

"Sam, I'm tired of playing gin rummy. Do you know of any other two-player games?"

"Have you ever played the game of nim?" Mohlar asked.

"Nope, how do you play it?"

"You start with twenty-one coins," Mohlar explained. "The first player can take away one, two, or three coins. Then the other player takes away one, two, or three coins. This process continues until one of the players takes away the last coin. The player who takes away the last coin wins."

"So who starts?" Gray asked as he counted his coins.

"Let's alternate who starts. You can start first," Mohlar suggested.

After Mohlar won all six games they played, Gray said, "I know that whoever takes away coins so that four coins remain always wins."

"That's correct. Now extend your thinking so you can be guaranteed to be in position where you can remove coins so that four coins remain."

"I see; you wanna be the one to remove coins so there's eight left," Gray said. "When your opponent takes one, two, or three coins away, you can pick up the right number of coins so that four are left."

"This is a game that the person who goes first can always win," Mohlar said. "Regardless of who goes first, your goal should always be to reduce the pile to a multiple of four; that is four, eight, twelve, sixteen, or twenty. Do you see how it works?"

"Yeah, I think so. Let's play a few games so I can be sure I know how to win."

After they played a few games, Gray knew how to win at nim.

TWENTY

At nine–fifteen that same night, a man parked his car on a dead–end street on the west side of Rochester. It was raining, but not hard. Because the moon and stars were not visible, it was very dark.

He pulled out his .22-caliber revolver and silencer from his pocket and placed them on the passenger seat. From a box next to the revolver, he grabbed a handful of bullets, counted out six, and returned the rest to the box. He inserted one bullet into each of the six chambers of the revolver, picked up the silencer and slid it onto the barrel of the revolver, and returned the revolver to his pocket.

He walked three blocks north of where he parked the car, turned left, and continued walking. He saw the house he was look-ing for: a large red house with three white pillars standing in a quiet street. He had been to this house several times before and always approached from the front.

But this time was different. He went around to the back of the house. He was startled when a dog barked, but was relieved to see that none of the neighbors paid attention.

Before realizing it, he was walking through a plush vegetable and flower garden on the east side of the backyard. He thought it would be a beautiful place to see in the daylight.

William Goldberg was inside the house, unaware that a man was approaching his back door. Goldberg was finishing off a bottle of wine and dozing when there was a knock at the door. The first knock was gentle, not hard enough to stir him. The next knock was loud. Goldberg patted his mouth with a white handkerchief and rose to his feet with effort. The knocking grew more persistent and the doorknob was turning when Goldberg answered the door.

The man entered the house and took off his shoes so he wouldn't leave any mud on the floor.

"I can't believe I'm looking at you," Goldberg said. "I wasn't expecting you for two more weeks."

"You told me that your wife plays bridge every other week, so I figured today would be as good a day to see you as two weeks from now."

"Don't do this again. Unilaterally changing our meeting time may have put me in a difficult situation. We're fortunate that meeting you tonight won't be a problem. Let's go to the library."

Although the library was quite large, actually expansive, it seemed crowded. There were bookshelves on three sides, a large desk with a computer in the south end of the room, a large television set with a VCR enclosed on the north end of the room, and a large file cabinet in the west end of the room.

As they entered the library, the man licked his lips, looked around, and said, "You sure have a lot of books. Why don't you keep your law books at your office?"

"Most of them are, but I do some of my work at home so I need these books here. And as you know, some books I don't want people to see. I feel they're more protected here. Did you bring the money?" Goldberg asked.

"Yes, but this will be the last payment. I figure I don't need Lewis Petroleum Company anymore."

"It makes sense to let the petroleum company go out of business; otherwise, you're only stealing from yourself. But what I don't understand is why you think this is the last payment. I expect that you'll continue to make semiannual payments in return for my silence."

"Part of what I was paying you for was the protection of the company books. When Krista examined last year's books, she figured out what I was doing. It was as if you had told her everything.

I figure the best way of keeping you silent," he said as he pulled his revolver from his pocket, "is to kill you."

The man raised the revolver and aimed it at Goldberg's head. He looked with calculating eyes into the terrified face of Goldberg.

"Hey, I'll take better care of these books," Goldberg quickly said as he backed away, stunned at what he saw. Misery and fright blurred his eyes as he said, "You know I won't tell anyone what I know."

"I'm going to make sure of that," the man said as he pulled the trigger. He hit his target and Goldberg fell to the floor. The man shot him twice more to ensure he was dead.

He took a paintbrush out of his pocket, dipped it into Goldberg's blood, and walked over to the south wall of the library. He wrote the following message in blood on the green wall:

Palestinians, seize your land!
Murder all Jews!

He went to the bookshelves and searched through the books. When he found what he was looking for, he removed them from the shelf. He walked out of the library, put his shoes back on, and left the house via the back door. Once out on the street he drew a long, deep breath of fresh air, cracked a smile, and felt he had eliminated a burden in his life.

———

At eleven that night Mohlar was awakened out of a deep sleep when the telephone rang.

"Hello, this is Elwood Luff. Am I speaking to Sam Mohlar?"

"Yes, what do you want?"

"I want you to help me investigate a homicide. How long will it take you to get to 132 Oak Street in Rochester?"

"About two hours. I don't think I can help you this time; I need to be in Buffalo by 8:30 tomorrow morning."

"You can probably make it back in time. If necessary, I'll give you a police escort."

"I'll be there as soon as possible."

It was still raining when Mohlar left his motel room. As Mohlar was driving toward Rochester, the rain became a drizzle and finally stopped.

When Mohlar arrived at the victim's home, he had the feeling he had been there before. The big house was illuminated with light coming out of every window. The light made policemen visible, both inside and outside the house.

When Mohlar got out of his car, Lieutenant Luff greeted him. Mohlar was surprised when Luff said, "The victim is an attorney named William Goldberg."

"I knew him," Mohlar replied. "I talked to him about the death of Krista Clark. How did Goldberg die?"

"He was shot three times. One bullet went through his head and two bullets through his chest."

"Do you know what the murder weapon was?"

"We know it was a small-caliber revolver. It'll take two or three hours to get a precise description of the gun. Would you give us an estimate of the time of death?"

Mohlar walked into the library and slowly made a 360-degree turn with his eyes, taking in as many details as possible. He examined the bullet holes in the body. Then Mohlar noted the temperature of the body, the temperature of the room, and the time. After doing some calculations, he said, "I'm ninety-five percent confident that he died at 9:45 p.m., give or take thirty minutes."

"So you're almost positive he was killed between 9:15 and 10:15 last night."

"That's correct. It appears that the murderer left a hate message," Mohlar said as he read what was painted on the wall.

"Obviously the murderer is anti-Semitic," Luff noted.

"Or he wants us to think he is," Mohlar said as he measured the height of the highest letter on the wall.

Then Mohlar went outside the house and looked around. He

said to himself, *If murderers knew how easy it is for homicide investigators to obtain information from footprints in muddy ground, they would never commit murders on rainy days. I'm fortunate that this murderer didn't think of that.* Mohlar carefully measured the size of the footprints and the distance between them.

After several hours of carefully examining the grounds, Mohlar returned to the library. He made a diligent and painstaking investigation of the contents of the library. He found Goldberg's checkbook but didn't note anything suspicious, such as any recent large deposits or withdrawals. He opened every desk drawer and looked at every document.

Meanwhile, officers came and went. A photographer came in and took pictures. An officer told Luff that a mortuary ambulance was outside waiting for clearance to remove the body. Mohlar told Luff that as far as he was concerned, they could remove Goldberg anytime.

When Mohlar looked over the bookshelves, he placed his left hand on his forehead and appeared to be deep in thought. Finally, he said to Luff, "Do you see anything interesting about the bookshelves?"

Luff thought for a few seconds and then answered, "No. Why do you ask?"

"I was just wondering if anything looked strange to you," Mohlar answered as he pulled a book from a bookshelf and quickly scanned the pages.

After Mohlar returned the book, he turned to Luff and asked, "Was there anyone in the house when Goldberg was shot?"

"No. His wife returned home at about 10:45 and discovered the body. She called us immediately."

Mohlar walked into the living room where he found Mrs. Goldberg crying. He said, "Mrs. Goldberg, I'm sorry about what has happened to your husband. My name is Sam Mohlar, and I've been asked to help the police with his murder investigation. Have you noticed anything missing from your home?"

She peered into his face with red and swollen eyes and answered, "No, I haven't."

"Would you come into the library with me?"

"Please, Mr. Mohlar, don't make me go into that room. The last time I was in that room I saw my dead husband on the floor with blood all over his body. It would be difficult for me to go back in that room."

"Let me try to get the information I'm looking for in another way. If you'd be so kind, Mrs. Goldberg, describe the books on the shelves in the library."

"I'm as familiar with the books in the library as I am with the palm of my hand. Do you want to know the title of each book, or the types of books and where they're located?"

"The latter, please."

"At the northeast end of the library are novels and plays. Do you want me to be any more specific than that?"

"That is specific enough," Mohlar answered. *This is an incredible woman, a woman with a detailed mind*, he said to himself.

"At the northwest end of the library are biographies and nonfiction stories. At the west side of the library are my husband's law books. At the southwest side are my husband's business clients' notebooks—"

"I want you to focus on that part of the library," Mohlar interrupted. "Were those shelves full or were there gaps on the shelves?"

"There were no gaps on those shelves. In fact, just the other day he said that he needed more room for those notebooks."

"It appears that some of those books were removed. If you were to see the shelf, could you identify the specific books that were missing?"

"No, I can't. That part of Bill's library was always changing. He was always adding new books that represented new clients and taking away old books that represented past clients."

"Thank you, Mrs. Goldberg, for your help."

Mohlar went back to the library and walked over to Luff, who was still investigating the contents of the room.

"I'd suggest that you have an officer make plaster casts of the footprints in the backyard," Mohlar said.

"Someone did that while you were talking to Mrs. Goldberg," Luff replied.

"Elwood, the pieces of this mystery are starting to fall into place. I'd like to stay here longer and help you with this investigation, but I must be in Buffalo in about an hour. Can you get me there quickly?"

"Yes, but I want to know who killed Goldberg. I think I know, but I want to see if you agree with me," Luff said.

"I'll tell you while we're traveling to Buffalo," Mohlar responded.

TWENTY-ONE

While Mohlar and Luff were heading west toward Buffalo, they discussed Goldberg's murder. Mohlar said, "Since there was no sign of a break–in, it appears that Goldberg knew the murderer. It may have also been that the murderer knew when Mrs. Goldberg would be out of the house."

Finally Luff came to a conclusion. "I think Darren Aderman killed Goldberg. It's well-known that he hated Jews. Besides, there's mounting evidence that he killed that chemist, Rubenstein. Maybe there's a connection between the homicides."

"And he particularly hated that Jew," Mohlar responded. "He felt that Goldberg had influenced his sister in excluding him from an inheritance he deserved." Mohlar paused briefly, then said, "But Aderman didn't kill Goldberg."

"Why do you say that?"

"Aderman is a man of average height, maybe slightly below average height. The person who killed Goldberg is very tall."

"How do you know he's tall?" Luff asked.

"I measured the footprints in the muddy vegetable garden in back of Goldberg's house. The prints were made from large feet. People who wear big shoes are usually tall."

"Maybe Aderman put large shoes over his other shoes in order to leave those prints and throw suspicion away from himself," Luff said.

"I still don't think Aderman killed Goldberg. I measured the distance between the footprints behind Goldberg's house. A man who is about seven feet tall made these footprints last night. Recall the height of the message on the wall. Either the message was written by a tall person or by someone who brought a chair or something to stand on. It's very unlikely that the killer took the time to bring something to stand on over to the wall."

Luff had to apply the brakes of his car, as traffic had suddenly become heavier. He turned on the siren and flashing lights of the police car so other cars would get out of his way.

"There are advantages to driving a police car," Luff chuckled. "So who do you think killed Goldberg?"

"I think Raymond Clark killed him. He certainly is very tall. But not only that, some books were missing from Goldberg's library, books of client records. Goldberg did legal work for Clark's plastic company. I bet you that if we could examine those books, we would know why Clark killed Goldberg.

"There's another reason I think Clark killed Goldberg. Some of the letters in the message were printed in unusual ways. For example, the letter 'Z' was made with a line drawn through it. People who do work in mathematics print 'Z' that way to distinguish it from the number '2.' I know Clark prints the capital letter 'Z' as I described."

"How do you know how Clark prints letters?"

"When Clark hired us to find his ex-chauffeur, Flood, he wrote out a contract for us to sign. When I read over the contract, I noticed the unusual way he prints some letters."

"In order to give the district attorney a chance at a conviction, we need to recover those missing books," Luff said. "He won't nail him on what you've told me."

"You're right. We've got to get those books."

Mohlar was very much relieved when he arrived at his apartment safely at 8:25. Luff drove at a speed that encouraged Mohlar to spend time in prayer, but at least he hadn't missed Gray's call. Mohlar and Luff went into his apartment and waited.

———

Gray arrived at Flood's house five minutes later. When he entered the room, Flood said, "Mr. Streeter, I'm glad you came. Did you bring your baseball cards with you?"

"Yeah, I did. Here're the ones I have from the 1950s."

After Flood looked over the cards Gray handed him, he said, "Some cards I'm looking for aren't here. Have any cards of Joe DiMaggio, Roy Campanella, or Pee Wee Reese?"

"I don't, but I know someone who does. Let me call him and I'll see if we can go over to his house and look at his cards."

"Please call him," Flood said, "but see if he'll come here."

As Gray was reaching for his cell phone, Flood pulled out his .357 magnum revolver and said, "Mr. Streeter—or should I say Mr. Gray—I'll tell you what to say to Mr. Mohlar. That is who you were going to call, isn't it?"

Gray was shocked to be looking down the barrel of a revolver. The hare had turned upon the hound, and the hare had the power. "Come on, man. Why are you pointing that gun at me?" Gray asked, as he tried to look puzzled instead of frightened.

"Tell me where the hundred grand is that you lifted from the moneybag."

Gray told him that Mohlar had found the moneybag and brought it to him. They each counted the money twice and each time counted out six hundred thousand dollars.

"I believe you're straight with me. I think Mohlar snatched a hundred grand before he showed you the moneybag."

"Mohlar is an honest man. I'm sure he gave Hamilton all the money he found."

"He'll give me the money after I confront him. I'll write out exactly what I want you to say to him."

"I'm not gonna call him. For all I know, you'll kill him. Maybe you're gonna kill me too."

"I'm not going to kill him. I just want the money. But if you don't call Mohlar, I'll put a bullet through your head."

"Well, you'll have to shoot me then 'cause I'm not gonna call him."

Flood forced Gray to tie his feet together. He took the revolver and placed a silencer on it. Flood tied Gray's hands behind his back. He then removed five of the six bullets. He spun the cylinder around and held the revolver to Gray's head.

"I've always enjoyed playing games," Flood said as he pulled back the hammer of the single-action revolver. "Unless you give Mohlar a call, I'll pull the trigger. The revolver may or may not fire because we don't know which chamber the bullet is in. If the revolver doesn't fire, I'll wait fifteen minutes and give you another chance to call Mohlar. This procedure will continue until you call Mohlar or the revolver fires. I hope you change your mind."

"Please give me a minute to think," Gray said as he closed his eyes.

"You got one minute. Change your mind or I'll pull the trigger."

Gray silently said to God, *Lord, I know I've turned my back on you many times. Jesus, I want you to know that right now I accept you as my Lord and Savior. Please forgive me of my sins. I hope you save me from this situation. I can't betray my friend. If I should call Sam and ask him over here, I'll put him in a dangerous situation. Please help . . .*

Gray didn't even finish the sentence before he heard the click of the revolver.

"You won fifteen more minutes of life," Flood said. "But I'm not impressed by your courage because chances are that the revolver would not fire. I hope you don't put yourself through this torture again."

When Gray was a child, his mother helped him memorize the twenty-third Psalm. Although he had not recited it in many years, he could remember every word of the Psalm. He then said to himself:

> The LORD is my shepherd, I shall not be in want. He makes me lie down in green pastures, he leads me beside quiet waters, he restores my soul. He guides me in the paths of righteousness for his name's sake. Even though I walk through the valley of the

shadow of death, I will fear no evil, for you are with me; your rod and your staff, they comfort me. You prepare a table before me in the presence of my enemies. You anoint my head with oil; my cup overflows. Surely goodness and love will follow me all the days of my life, and I will dwell in the house of the LORD forever.

Gray continued to pray until Flood walked into the room. Flood said, "I hope you've changed your mind. The decision seems simple to me. If you call Mohlar, you'll live. If you don't call him, you'll die. That seems to be a no-brainer."

"I don't trust you. I can't put my friend in danger; I can't betray a friend."

"Why don't you trust me? If you ask Mohlar to come here, I won't kill either of you. I give you my word."

"I don't trust you," Gray repeated.

As Flood put the revolver to Gray's head, Gray closed his eyes. Flood pulled back the hammer, pulled the trigger, and again the revolver didn't fire. Gray opened his eyes and sighed.

This mind torture was repeated three more times.

"This time we know the revolver will fire. This is your last chance to live," Flood said as he raised the revolver to Gray's head.

Gray quickly said, "Let's play a game. If you win, I'll call Mohlar. If I win, I live."

"That's fine with me, but I want to choose the game."

"I think we should agree on the game," Gray replied. "Let's alternate suggesting games until we agree on one to play."

"Okay," Flood said.

Flood's first suggestion was chess, but Gray said that he wasn't a good chess player. Then the detective suggested pool, but Flood said that he didn't have a pool table in the house. Gray rejected Flood's next suggestion of backgammon.

Then the detective suggested the game of nim. Flood asked

how to play the game. Gray explained the rules of the game, hoping Flood would agree to play.

Flood agreed to play but said that he wanted to be able to make the first move. The detective said, "I think I should make the first move, since I'm playing for my life and you're playing for a phone call."

"Nah, man, I should go first," Flood replied. "Besides, I'm the one with the gun."

"Let the game begin," Gray conceded, thinking he'd win anyway.

Flood counted out twenty-one coins and placed them on a table between the two of them. Flood started the game by removing one coin, leaving twenty on the table. Thus Gray could not take control of the game on the next move.

"Take away three coins," Gray instructed Flood since he was still tied up.

Flood again took away one coin, leaving sixteen coins on the table. Gray could still not take control of the game with his next move.

Maybe Flood will take away one coin on every move, Gray thought to himself.

"Take away two coins," Gray said, leaving fourteen coins on the table. Immediately Flood took away two coins, leaving twelve coins on the table. Gray was still unable to take control.

Gray began to think that Flood's moves were more than just lucky moves. *Maybe Flood knows how to play this game.*

"Take away one coin," the detective said as small beads of sweat appeared above his eyebrows. His breathing became labored.

Flood continued playing the game perfectly as he took away three coins, leaving eight coins on the table.

Perspiration began speckling Gray's forehead; he knew time was running out. But Flood was calm, cool and confident.

Gray said, "Take away two coins. There're now six coins left on the table."

Immediately Flood observed, "Now, I have you." He quickly removed two coins from the table, leaving four coins.

The game was essentially over. No matter what Gray did, Flood would win on the next move. The detective said, "Take away one coin."

Flood picked up the last three coins and won the game.

"I'm a man of my word," Gray said. "Let me read over what you want me to say to Mohlar."

TWENTY-TWO

Gray's eyes opened wide as he watched Flood grab a knife off a table. He gave a sigh of relief as he watched Flood cut the ropes binding him to a chair. After Flood cut the ropes around his wrists, Gray moved his hands back and forth, trying to get his blood circulating.

Flood handed him a sheet of paper and said, "Study this so you know exactly what you're to say to Mohlar."

While Gray was studying the paper, Flood went to the refrigerator and pulled out a can of root beer. "Make the phone call now," Flood said as he pulled the metal tab off the top of the can.

While Gray was dialing the phone, Flood put the can of root beer and the metal tab on the kitchen table. He then put five more bullets into the revolver.

At 10:15 a.m., Mohlar's cell phone rang. Mohlar took a swallow of ginger ale and said into the phone, "Hello."

"This is Michael Streeter," Gray replied. "I am talking to someone who is interested in buying your Joe DiMaggio, Pee Wee Reese, and Roy Campanella baseball cards. Could you come over to his house this morning and show him what you have?"

"Yes, I want to show him my cards."

"Good. He lives at 395 Kitty Avenue in Buffalo. If you are going east on Ninth Avenue, drive past the Monroe Mall. The fourth intersection past the mall is Kitty Avenue. Turn right onto Kitty Avenue. The first house on the left is green. Drive past this house and the next house on the left, which is blue. The next house on the left, which is a yellow house, is his."

"I'll be there shortly," Mohlar replied.

After Mohlar hung up the phone, he said to Luff, "I know Ken is in trouble. First, Ken was to call me to ask if they could come here. Instead he asked me to go to Flood's house. Second, Ken is colorblind. He can't tell a green house from a blue house from a yellow house, but he described three houses as having these colors on the street. Third, Ken can't speak that many sentences without making a grammatical error. Flood forced him to say exactly what he said on the phone."

"I know the head of the homicide division of the Buffalo Police Department, Pat Charles," Luff said. "I'll call him and see if he can help us."

"Hello, Pat, this is Elwood Luff. I'm in Buffalo and I'd like your help in arresting a man suspected of a homicide in Rochester. He's thought to be armed and dangerous."

"Sure, we'll help you out. We'll send you four men," Charles said.

"That should be sufficient help. Please send them to the intersection of Ninth and Kitty Avenue as soon as possible."

———

After Gray hung up the phone, he walked over to the kitchen table and sat across from Flood. He pulled a gun on Gray. With his elbows remaining on the table, Gray lifted his arms as a sign of surrender.

At that moment, the front doorbell rang. When Flood looked toward the door, Gray quickly lowered his arms, grabbed the metal tab off the table, and put it up his sleeve.

"What should I do with you?" Flood asked Gray, not expecting a reply.

Flood went over to the kitchen counter and picked up a large dark blue bandanna handkerchief. He tied it over Gray's mouth, led him into the bedroom, and locked the door. The front doorbell continued to ring.

Gray pulled the metal tab out of his sleeve and slipped it into the crack in the door. He wiggled it until he felt the curve of the lock. He slid it back and it released.

Meanwhile Flood answered the door. The mailman said, "I have a registered letter for Joseph Masters. Are you Mr. Masters?"

"Yes, I am,"

"Please sign on this line," the mailman said while pointing to where he wanted Flood to sign.

After Flood closed the door, he turned around and saw Gray ready to open the back door. "Freeze!" he said while pulling his revolver out of his pocket.

Gray immediately stopped. Flood walked over to Gray and pulled the handkerchief from his mouth. Flood raised his revolver, pointed it at Gray's head, and pulled back the hammer.

"I'm sorry, Mr. Gray, but I'm going to kill you. I actually like you, but you're worth ten grand to me dead, and you're worth nothing to me alive."

"But you promised that you wouldn't hurt me if I called my friend."

"I lied to you about that. You might be interested to know that I've played the game of nim before, but I didn't know what it was called. Once you explained the rules of the game to me, I recalled playing the game before. I knew I'd win the game if I made the first move."

"Before you kill me, tell me if you murdered Krista Clark."

With a look of surprise, Flood asked, "How do you know Krista Clark?"

"I heard of her death through her husband. He told me that he suspected you of killing her."

"I killed Mrs. Clark. It wasn't hard to do, since I loathed her."

"How did you get into the house that night?"

"Two days before I killed Mrs. Clark, I met Mr. Clark at a park in Rochester. He gave me his key, his wife's revolver, a suicide note, and five grand. The night after I killed her, I met him at the same park. I was to give him his key and he was to give me another five grand but he bamboozled me out of the money. After I gave him his key, he reached in his pocket. Instead of pulling out my money, he pulled out a revolver. I knocked the gun out of his hand and ran. He took a shot at me but missed. I guess he'd feel safer with me dead. But anyway, I knew I had to leave Rochester in a hurry last March, or he'd hunt me down and kill me."

"Do you know why he wanted his wife dead?"

"He didn't tell me why he wanted me to kill her, but he did say it had to be done on Saturday, March 26. He had a good alibi and he knew my daughter would be out of town that day. He knew I wouldn't do it if my daughter was in the house."

"Why did he choose you to kill his wife?"

"He knew I didn't like his wife, so killing her wouldn't be difficult for me. Somehow, and I wish I knew how, he found out I did a hit about a year ago. He used that information as leverage to get me to do the hit on Mrs. Clark.

"I've something funny to tell you. I took the hundred thousand dollars out of the moneybag Mohlar found. Andrew Hamilton was supposed to pick up the bag, but Mohlar beat him to it. When Mohlar returned the remaining money to Randy Hamilton, he was convinced that Mohlar and possibly you were holding out on him. So Hamilton hired me to kill both of you. It's like I'm getting a twenty thousand-dollar bonus for stealing the money. Of course, I wouldn't be telling you all this if there were any chance that you'd tell someone else. Since I'm going to kill you now, there's no possible way."

"Could I make one last request before you kill me?" Gray asked. "May I go to the bathroom?"

Flood quickly granted his request because cleaning up Gray's blood in the bathroom would be easier than other places in the house.

After taking a few steps toward the bathroom, Gray turned quickly to strike Flood, but Flood was alert and pulled the trigger.

Even though the bullet passed through Gray's lung, he was still able to knock the gun out of Flood's hand. He grabbed Flood and wrestled him to the floor. Gray was weakening fast and Flood was able to push him aside. Flood quickly picked up the revolver and shot him two more times. Gray inhaled his last breath of air.

Flood pulled a large sleeping bag out of his closet and put Gray's bloody body into the sleeping bag. He then pulled the body toward the back door of his house.

———

Mohlar and Luff arrived at the intersection of Ninth and Kitty. Mohlar waited for the Buffalo police officers to arrive while Luff scouted out Flood's house.

When Luff returned, he said, "I want you to meet Flood. Go to the front door and knock. As soon as he opens the door, get out of the way and two of the police officers will make the arrest. Flood may try to run out the back door. If he does, I'll be waiting for him with the other two police officers."

Soon the four Buffalo police officers arrived. Luff informed them of his plans for arresting Flood.

The six men started walking toward Flood's house. Mohlar and two of the officers walked down the street while Luff and the other two officers walked behind the houses.

When they were close to Flood's house, all six men saw Flood dragging a sleeping bag out of the back door of his house. Suddenly, they saw a tall man appear from behind some bushes. He crouched, raised a revolver, took aim, and shot. Smoke was seen coming from the gun, but no sound was heard. Flood immediately fell to the ground.

Luff cried out, "Clark, drop your gun and raise your arms."

Clark turned and fired his gun toward Luff. The bullet missed everyone. Clark then turned and ran away from the six men who were running toward him.

One of the police officers near Luff yelled, "Stop, or I'll shoot!" But Clark continued to run.

The officer raised his revolver and shot. Clark immediately fell to the ground.

Mohlar and the two officers with him stopped to check on Flood. He was dead. Mohlar picked up and opened the sleeping bag. He wept when he saw the dead body of his friend and business partner.

Everyone ran over to check on Clark. Luff, while placing his shirt on Clark's wound, said, "He's alive but needs medical attention soon."

Mohlar quickly took his cell phone out of his pocket and dialed 911.

"Please call an ambulance to 395 Kitty Avenue," he said. "A man has been shot but is still alive."

TWENTY-THREE

It was ten minutes until ten o'clock in the morning when Mohlar arrived at a large Catholic church on the east side of Rochester. He was amazed to see so many people already gathered over an hour before the funeral services for Gray were scheduled to begin. He remembered Gray saying that both his parents came from large families.

As he looked over the crowd, he was surprised to see his friend, Kay Townsend. He walked slowly toward her, weaving through the crowd. She smiled when he was near her.

"When did you get out of the hospital?" Mohlar inquired.

"I was released yesterday."

"How are you feeling?" Mohlar asked.

"I'm okay, but I tire easily. Have you had any more occurrences of that nightmare you told me about?"

"My dreams have been wonderful ever since I became a Christian. Thanks for your concern."

Suddenly, Kay's eyes became large. Her voice sank as she said, "Sam, I can hardly believe what I'm seeing. Check out the back of the church."

Mohlar immediately saw Scott. He was one of the tallest men in the back of the church and the only one with no hair on his head. "Since Scott is here, Randy Hamilton is probably nearby. Do you see him, Kay?"

Kay took a few seconds to look around and said, "Yes, he's ahead and to the left of Scott."

"I see Hamilton now too. They'll try to kill me if they see me."

"Sam, too many people are around for him to try anything here."

"He's hoping to follow me out of here. I suggest that you leave before the service, and I'll leave after. I don't think they'll give you trouble; they came here to find me. But be careful. If they see you, they may want to kidnap you like they did before. Please meet me at this address at one this afternoon," Mohlar said while handing Kay his business card.

"I'm scared. I want to leave with you now or after the service. Leaving after the service would be better because we can take advantage of the crowd," Kay said.

"You're in danger when you're with me. You'll be safe if you leave soon. They won't risk losing me by following you."

Mohlar put his hands on hers; they were trembling like a leaf. "Relax, Kay. We both know God is with us."

"Be careful, Sam."

They looked upward at the ceiling as if they were in prayer. After they held each other's hands for a couple of minutes, Mohlar and Kay separated. They sat on opposite sides of the church, Kay sitting closest to the exit.

Kay sat near four of Gray's cousins, all young and big. She whispered to them, "A few days ago, the large bald-headed man in the back of the church and his boss—the short man standing beside him—kidnapped me. I don't feel safe with those two men here. Would you men please escort me to my car so I know I'll be safe?"

They all nodded their heads, indicating they would escort her to her car. Then she whispered, "Ken Gray's business partner is also here. He's the bearded man in the brown suit sitting on the left side of the church. He's in the sixth pew from the front and at the far end. Those two men came here to give him trouble. Would you make sure he gets out of here safely?"

One of Gray's cousins whispered, "I see who you're referring to. We'll make sure both of you are safe."

Before the funeral service started, Kay rose from her seat and her four escorts also rose. She walked quickly but nonchalantly out of the church.

Scott walked out of the church ten feet behind Kay and Gray's four cousins. Kay turned and said, "That's the man who kidnapped me."

As Gray's cousins moved toward Scott, he reached in his pocket and started to pull out a revolver. Three of Gray's cousins quickly grabbed him and threw him to the ground. The gun dropped on the grass. The fourth cousin picked up the gun and put it in his suit pocket. He turned to Kay and said, "Quickly, get out of here! We'll take care of this guy."

While Kay got in her car and drove away, Gray's four cousins beat Scott until he was unconscious. They left Scott lying in his own blood and went back into the church.

One of them took a seat behind Mohlar and whispered, "Were you Ken's business partner?"

Mohlar answered, "Yes."

"A pretty girl said she may be in danger from two men in the church. My three brothers and I made sure she left the church safely. In the process of roughing up the big man, I removed his gun. She said you might also be in danger from these same two men. The four of us will stay close to you during the funeral service. After the service, we'll guard you until you get into your car. We'll see to it that they don't follow you."

"Thanks," Mohlar replied. "Here is a hundred dollars to show my appreciation for helping both the pretty girl and me."

"Put the money back in your pocket. Let's say we are doing this in memory of our cousin, Ken."

Mohlar pointed to the back of the church and said, "Look who just walked in." Gray's cousin turned his head and saw Scott staggering into the back of the church. Mohlar could see cuts all over his face.

"I'll keep an eye on him," Gray's cousin responded to the detective.

After Gray's funeral service, Hamilton and a scarred Scott rose to follow Mohlar out of the church. But Gray's four cousins walked over to them and told them to sit down and relax for a few minutes. In order to enforce their command, Gray's cousin, who had picked up the revolver, pulled it out of his suit pocket.

He said, "At the end of the five minutes I'll give you back your revolver after I remove the bullets."

Mohlar drove directly to his office after the funeral. He knew he was going to have to give up using the office. It would be only a matter of time when Hamilton would find it. Besides, it would be too painful to come to the office and not see Ken Gray there.

Mohlar said to himself, *Lord, you know I don't want to be a private detective anymore, especially without Ken. Please help me decide what I'm going to do next. What work should I, or can I do? Maybe I should read the Bible for guidance, but that's a big book and I don't know where to look. Lord, I'm going to randomly open the Bible and start reading. Please guide me to a passage that will help me decide what kind of work I should pursue.*

Mohlar opened the Bible to Acts 8: 30 and read:

Then Philip ran up to the chariot and heard the man reading Isaiah the prophet. "Do you understand what you are reading?" Philip asked. "How can I," he said, "unless someone explains it to me?" So he invited Philip to come up and sit with him.

Mohlar concluded that God was telling him to be a teacher. Philip helped that man understand what he was reading. Similarly, he could help people understand mathematical concepts.

Mohlar glanced at the clock and noticed that Kay would arrive in twenty minutes, which gave him just enough time to update the file on the Clark case.

He heard a soft knock at the door. When he opened the door and saw Kay standing there, he smiled and said, "I didn't expect you yet."

"You said to meet you here at one o'clock," she replied. "I'm right on time."

"I forgot my clock is twenty minutes slow. Come into my office."

"Did you have any trouble leaving the church?" Kay asked.

"No. The same men who helped you also helped me. I'd suggest that you and your sister attend a college outside this area. Hamilton may continue to be a threat to you."

"I'll ask Jenny where she'd like to go. After what I've been through this past week, I'm sure we'll go somewhere far away from here. I'm sorry about what happened to Ken. I imagine his death is devastating to you."

"I just can't imagine my life without ever seeing Ken again. But I felt that same way after my father died. After he died, I went through an intense, but brief time of grieving. Hopefully this time my grieving will be brief. It certainly is intense."

"Are you going to look for another partner for your detective business? If you are, I'd suggest checking to see if any of the four men who helped us would like to get into the business."

"I'm going to give up the detective business. It just won't be the same without Ken."

"So what do you think you'll do?"

"Just before you arrived, I was reading the Bible. As I was reading, I sensed that God was telling me that he wants me to be a teacher. With a Ph.D. in mathematics, I should be able to teach at a college or university somewhere."

"Maybe we'll end up at the same college," Kay said as Mohlar set the clock to the correct time. "Are you finished with the case you've been working on?"

"I'm finished with that case, a very interesting case indeed."

"Can you tell me about it?"

Expecting that Mohlar would tell her about the case, Kay sat in a chair. She pulled her feet under her, put her elbows on her knees, and rested her chin on her hands.

Mohlar popped open a pair of sodas and gave one to her. He

sank into his swivel chair, turned to face her, and said, "Last March, a man by the name of Raymond Clark hired Ken and me to locate his ex-chauffeur, Richard Flood. Clark told us he believed Flood murdered his wife. Actually, he hired his chauffeur to kill his wife, and he wanted us to find him so he could kill him."

"Why did he want someone to kill his wife?" she asked.

"That's a long story that started when Raymond Clark and, at that time, Krista Aderman were in college. When they graduated from college, they were engaged to be married. They both obtained jobs in Krista's family plastic business. Soon after they started working, she broke off her engagement to him. They both continued to work for the plastic company.

"He was in charge of ordering the supplies that were needed in the manufacturing of plastic. Thinking he no longer was going to marry into wealth, he thought of a way of embezzling company funds. He established a bank account for the Lewis Petroleum Company, a nonexistent company. He periodically placed orders to this company to buy their petroleum. Even though the Aderman Plastic Company never received any petroleum from the Lewis Petroleum Company, Aderman punctually paid the bills and the money would be put into the bank account. Anytime Clark wanted money, he withdrew money from that account. About two years after Clark established the bank account, Raymond and Krista Clark were married. Raymond Clark continued to embezzle the company even though he married the daughter of the CEO of the company.

"Last March, Krista's brother, Darren, told her that he wanted some petroleum from the Lewis Petroleum Company. He said his chemist, David Rubenstein, wanted it for his research. He said he looked for it, but couldn't find any. So Krista looked at the company books and found that her husband had recently ordered some of their oil and it had been delivered and paid for. So she investigated and found out that there was no such company as the Lewis Petroleum Company. Then she knew that her husband embezzled from her company for years.

"When Krista informed him that she knew all about his embezzlement of company funds, she expelled him from their house. She also told him that she was going to see her lawyer, William Goldberg, and change her will. She was going to leave Clark nothing. Her entire estate was going to be left to her best friend, Marlo Shaw.

"Then Clark decided to hire Flood to kill his wife. He wanted Flood to kill her before she changed her will. Do you recall when we were eating dinner a week ago Tuesday, I received a call to investigate a homicide in Rochester?"

"I remember that call," she answered.

"The victim was Rubenstein. He became so frustrated with not having Lewis's oil, he decided to contact the oil company directly. When he discovered the company didn't exist, he shared the news with Clark. Clark knew he couldn't allow Rubenstein to tell anyone else, so he killed him.

"But Clark didn't stop killing people with the murder of the chemist. William Goldberg, the company lawyer, had blackmailed Clark for years because he also knew Clark was embezzling the company. Clark became furious when his wife found out about him and he blamed Goldberg for her discovery. So Clark murdered Goldberg. And when we found Flood for Clark, he killed Flood too."

"How do you know that this is what happened?" she asked.

"After Clark shot Flood, he tried to run away. But a police officer shot him and he fell to the ground. He was taken to the hospital and made a complete deathbed confession.

"It's interesting that Clark wanted to confess to killing the chemist. He knew that his brother-in-law, Darren Aderman, was going to be indicted for the murder of Rubenstein. He had known Aderman for many years and had always liked him. He didn't want him to be convicted of a crime he didn't commit."

Kay looked at the watch on her wrist and said, "I need to be going soon because I have a doctor's appointment."

Mohlar suddenly thought, *I'll never find another girl like Kay. She has everything I've ever looked for in a woman. She's beautiful and intelligent. She loves her family and seems to like me. I'd like to have children, and she'd be a good mother for them. I'm going to ask her to marry me.*

Just as he was about to speak, Mohlar thought, *I shouldn't. First, I can't support her. I don't have a job and I don't have a lot of money in the bank. Second, I don't fit into her plans. She wants to go to college. She won't have time for me. And third, she doesn't know me well enough to accept my proposal. No one accepts a proposal from someone that she has known for twelve days.*

Then Kay thought, *I wonder why Sam isn't saying anything. This might be the last time I'll ever see him. I can't stand the thought of never seeing him again. Haven't these last twelve days meant anything to him?*

Finally, she said, "I want to give you my new phone number before I leave.

As she wrote the number on a slip of paper, Mohlar said, "Since we met, and despite all the suffering we both have been through, I've never been happier."

"I feel the same way. Please keep in touch, Sam."

"I will," Mohlar promised.

REFERENCES

1 Psalm 23: 4
2 Psalm 91: 5
3 Psalm 91: 9–11
4 John 14: 1–4